Big Deal at Whistle Stop

Big Deal at Whistle Stop

by

Maurice L. Gimbel

With Jane B. Altschuler

Chaucer Press Books

An Imprint of Richard Altschuler & Associates, Inc.

New York

Distributed by University Press of New England
Hanover and London

ISBN-13: 978-1-884092-17-6

ISBN-10: 1-884092-17-9

Library of Congress Control Number: 2011929231

CIP data for this book are available from the Library of Congress

Chaucer Press Books is an imprint of
Richard Altschuler & Associates, Inc.

Cover Design: Josh Garfield

Printed in the United States of America

Distributed by University Press of New England
1 Court Street
Lebanon, New Hampshire 03766

Publisher's Preface

Big Deal at Whistle Stop by Maurice L. Gimbel originally came to my attention in 1992 as an early draft of a screenplay. I was immediately taken by the story—and especially by its unique "twist." I arranged to meet Mr. Gimbel in the hope of developing his screenplay for a feature film that I intended to produce, and shortly after our meeting I optioned the property.

Mr. Gimbel, in his late 70s when we met, was a longtime resident of New York and devotee and chronicler of the colorful and artistic world of Greenwich Village. I learned that he had published his poetry and songs before trying his hand at screenplay writing. Some of his songs were recorded by Morgana King, Solomon Burke, Doris Duke, and Buddy Greco. Bob Dylan recorded Mr. Gimbel's "Sidewalks, Fences and Walls," co-written with Swamp Dogg (Jerry Williams, Jr.), for inclusion on Dylan's 1987 album "Down in the Groove." While it did not get released on that album, the rare Dylan recording of Mr. Gimbel's song has since become a collector's item.

From my first reading of *Big Deal at Whistle Stop,* there was no question of Mr. Gimbel's ability to apply his artistry with words and penchant for satire to spin a unique Western tale with an unusually complex hero. Mr. Gimbel and I worked together to create a second draft that I showed to the head of production of a major studio. Duly impressed, he invited me to seek a director from a group the studio was interested in backing—a producing task I gladly pursued.

With several directors interested, two important events occurred that made it necessary to set the project aside—as so often happens in the motion picture industry. First, the interested studio was purchased by another company, which caused the production head who was working with me on *Big Deal at Whistle Stop* to leave the company; and then Mr. Gimbel became ill, and sadly passed away on September 11, 1994.

Subsequently, I purchased the rights to the property from Mr. Gimbel's estate. I was advised by the Writer's Guild of America's lawyer, given the work I had done with Mr. Gimbel, to take credit for any future drafts, while always giving credit for the original story and first draft to Mr. Gimbel. Using the lawyer's guidelines, I wrote another draft of the screenplay, which I called *Arizona Adams*.

In 2010, while our publishing company was planning its 2011 list of new book publications, we decided that the powerful satire in *Big Deal at Whistle Stop* was so delicious and pertinent to today's headline-grabbing boardroom shenanigans that it deserved to be published for all to enjoy.

To craft this novelization of Mr. Gimbel's *Big Deal at Whistle Stop* screenplay, I have incorporated unique elements from my *Arizona Adams* screenplay, as well as created new plot details; background information about Jim Courtney, the main character, and his family members; descriptions of other characters; and additional dialog necessary to make Mr. Gimbel's original work read in a novelistic way.

Jane B. Altschuler
New York, NY
April 2011

Prologue

A desert morning is one of the most peaceful times on Earth. Just after the turn of the twentieth century, the American West was beginning to catch up with the development in the big Eastern cities. Businessmen and entrepreneurs were looking to the West to capitalize on the wide open spaces and to seek their fortunes. Mostly, it was the railroad that brought these visionaries and tycoons to the Arizona Territory. At that time, the railroad made the great link to the East. The railroad ruled.

Chapter 1

The morning sun glints on a passenger train heading peacefully across the Arizona desert. On the side of each passenger car, in bold, black letters are the words CURTAIN RAIL LINES. Inside, the passengers are looking out of the windows at the hot, dry desert. The conductor calls out, "Reedville, next stop."

A passenger wipes his sweaty face with a big handkerchief and calls out, "Conductor, how many more stations to Whistle Stop?"

"Five. Good two hours more, sir."

"Thanks." The passenger looks out the window. Suddenly, the look on his face begins to register fear as he spots something moving in the distance, and then shots ring out. "Oh, Jesus."

About ten men on horses, with handkerchief masks covering their faces, are galloping full tilt straight for the train, firing rifles and six-guns. An athletic-looking man, dressed in black, is leading the attack. He's known as Arizona Adams. Two of his men gallop at top speed alongside the engine car, point their guns at the engineer, and the train slows and jerks to a stop. They guard the engine car, while Adams and the rest of his men quickly mount into the cars along the length of the train.

Arizona Adams enters a passenger car followed by two gang members, Grady and Sage. "Please stay calm, folks. The worst that will happen to you is that we'll be collecting a small fine from you for riding a train of the Curtain Rail Lines—twenty-five dollars per passenger." He motions to his men. "You two start collecting at the other end of the car." Holding up his gun to cover them, Arizona advises the passengers in a loud, but calm, voice. "Just drop the money into our hats as we reach you."

The passengers do so, some in nervous haste, some reluctantly. One mutters, "Last time I'll ride this train."

Arizona tips his hat as he collects the fines. "Thank you. Thank you, kindly. Much obliged."

The bored train conductor leans against the back of the car, yawns, then shakes his head resignedly, but does nothing when Sage, a scruffy looking but genial man, heads toward him calling out, "I'll check the other car, Arizona." The conductor steps aside for the outlaw.

Grady Profit, the other outlaw, continues collecting from the rear of the car. He is older than Arizona Adams, a lot tougher, and very pushy. Grady stops by a couple in their seventies with a very civilized manner. His eyes widen as he spots an expensive looking ring on the woman's finger. "Nice lookin' ring there, lady. You sure take good care of your princess, pop. I'd 'preciate it, lady, if you'd just slip it off and let me see it up close." A look of fear crosses the woman's face, while her husband makes a fuss about clearing his throat. Arizona, glancing up, sees what is going on.

"Yo!" Grady looks at Arizona, annoyed. "Go tell Purdy to hurry it up in the express car."

Grady glances at the ring, then back to Arizona. The look in his eyes says that the only thing stopping him from taking on his boss is a good deal of fear. He stomps off angrily. The woman is relieved. "Thank you, sir. You're a gentleman."

Arizona tips his hat. "I appreciate that, ma'am. Still gonna request you folks to pay your fines, though, if you don't mind." He collects their fines and goes on down the aisle. He stops in front of a dandy, impeccably dressed in fashionable Eastern clothes, with large, flashing rings on his fingers. "Would you mind letting me see your hands, sir?"

The dandy isn't looking for trouble. "My hands, why certainly, sir. Yessir!"

While inspecting the dandy's ring-bedecked hands, Arizona says, "Beautiful manicure! I can see a gentleman like you never had to string wire or dig post holes, now, did you?"

Confused, the dandy says, "Uh, no, sir."

Arizona says cordially, "So we'll give you a special fine of fifty dollars. All right with you?"

"Yessir, it's fine, fine!"

With a smile in his voice, Arizona says, "Oh, so you agree your fine is fine?"

The passenger, getting his point, digs frantically in his wallet while saying, "Yes, the fine is fine," and hands over the bills.

Arizona tips his hat again. "Thank you kindly, sir." He proceeds down the aisle stopping in front of a burly young fellow in work clothes. "Twenty-five bucks fine, pard."

The young fellow looks up, scared. "I'm sorry, sir, I ain't got but two bucks left."

"Been partyin'?"

"No, it ain't that, sir. It's just I ain't workin' right now. Goin' to Whistle Stop. Heard they might need somebody does my kinda work."

Arizona is curious now. "What kinda work might that be?"

The young man eases into the conversation. "Blacksmithin'."

"Blacksmithing. Good luck with that. So, short twenty-three bucks, are ya? Might be able to do something 'bout that." Arizona calls to the dandy, "Do you think you could call on your generous nature, sir, to lend this young fellow twenty-three dollars for the time being?"

The dandy is holding his hands up in the air, then reaches for his wallet again. "Oh, it would be a privilege, sir." He digs frantically into his wallet, fishes out the money, and hands it to Arizona.

He shakes the dandy's hand and says, "God will reward you, sir. And this young fellow here will pay you back if it takes the rest of his life. Right, young fella?"

The burly young fellow enters into the joke, saying, "If it takes the rest of my borned days. Thank you very kindly."

Arizona finishes collecting the fines. He sticks his head out a window and whistles shrilly between his teeth.

Hearing his signal, the gang members jump off the train and mount their horses. Arizona joins them and they hightail it towards hilly ground in the distance, carrying small sacks of coins and paper money. As they ride off, the train starts to move again. Inside the car the passengers, in a mixture of fear and relief, crowd to the windows to watch the gang disappear.

The burly young fellow says, "Lucky for them I warn't carryin' my six-gun! I'da put some new notches on it, I can tell you!" Some of the other male passengers join in.

"Yeah, me, too!"

"Dead right!"

The conductor looks around the car, asking, "Everybody okay?"

The elderly man says, "Yeah, everybody but him." He gestures toward the Eastern dandy who is stretched out inertly across his seat.

The conductor puts his ear to his chest, then looks up. "He ain't hurt, just fainted is all. Somebody pour some whiskey into him."

A passenger produces a bottle and pours it down the dandy's throat. He sits bolt upright, sputtering and choking in a panic. "Finc! Finc!" Then he realizes that the outlaws are gone.

The conductor shakes his head at the man. "Folks, in case yer wonderin', you have just had the privilege of bein' robbed by the derndest bunch of desperados that ever blew smoke off a gun barrel. You've heard of Butch Cassidy and the Wild Bunch up Utah way. Well, here we got Arizona Adams and the Odd Bunch. These fellas never rob stagecoaches, banks or other trains—just the trains of the Curtain Rail Lines."

One passenger yells out, "How come?" Another yells, "Why is that?"

The conductor settles into his story. "Well, it all started a long time ago when Mr. Joseph Curtain, the owner of this line, wanted to run tracks across the ranches and cattle lands around here. He found a legal loophole so's he wouldn't have to pay a plugged nickel for the properties. He got away with it. The son of one of the fifteen or twenty ranchers who lost everything and went bankrupt sent out an anonymous letter vowing to avenge his family's loss— and the loss of every rancher along the Curtain Rail Lines' tracks. Then nothin' happened until the last few years. You just seen how he's been tryin' to make good on that vow. We believe that feller is the one you just met up with, Arizona Adams. One of the nicest bandits you'll ever have the pleasure of meeting, and he never hurts a soul."

The dandy, still recovering, calls out indignantly, "I don't care if he's nice, why isn't he in jail?"

Chapter 2

In a mountainous, concealed canyon, Arizona Adams and his men, riding single file, take a very narrow path past a jut of rock, then approach their hideout. They dismount and unmask. Arizona, a clean-shaven, ruggedly good-looking man about thirty years old, stands aside as Diz, Corky, Purdy, Gyp, Ben, Hogan and Jack—all rough-looking types between twenty-five and forty years old—follow Sage and Grady into the cabin. Arizona takes a look around to make sure they weren't followed and then enters. He sets his sack of money on a wooden table. "Alright Sage, count it out and divvy it up."

The others set their sacks on the table and old Sage counts the money. "Twenty-five, fifty, seventy-five."

Arizona watches for a minute then makes up his mind about Grady Profit, whose eyes are glued to the money. "Grady, you're gonna have to watch yourself."

Grady, whose weathered face is as tough looking as he acts, looks up like he's ready to draw his gun and growls, "Watch what?" Sage stops counting and puts his hand on his gun. The room grows quiet.

Arizona calmly replies, "Since you're pretty new to the gang, I'll tell you my rules one last time. No rough stuff with the passengers or the trainmen, and a twenty-five buck fine up to a maximum of fifty bucks, nothing more. If you can't handle that, it might be best if you clear out and hook up with another outfit. Got it?"

Grady gives Arizona a strong stare. Arizona stares him down. Grady turns away muttering to himself and rolls a cigarette, but holds back from any confrontation, mostly for fear of Arizona. Arizona keeps his eye on him for a few seconds more, as Grady twists the ends of his smoke and lights up. He then turns and walks into the back room. Sage, satisfied that Grady has been put in his place, returns to the counting, and portions out the money.

*

Arizona re-enters dressed in light-colored riding pants, a white shirt, a raw-hide vest, and a light tan hat. He says, "There y'are, boys. Don't give it all to the poker sharks and the dance hall ladies. Make it last 'til the next time."

"Don't know about that, boss, I sure like the ladies," blurts Diz.

"Shur thing, he'll be broke by Friday," says Corky.

Purdy chimes in with a laugh, "And ain't you the one to talk, Corky. We all know how much you love to dip your dinger and wet your whistle."

Corky turns on him. "Ah reckon ah do, jes like you, you old fart." The men crack up laughing.

Arizona laughs with them. "You're in charge, Sage. Keep 'em out of trouble."

"Aw shucks, boss, just what I need is to be watchin' over a bunch of horny toads." Sage winks at Arizona and they shake hands warmly. Grady watches, taking the last drag from his cigarette. Arizona takes nothing for himself from the pile of money, gives Grady one last hard look, and leaves the hideout.

Grady exhales, takes a few steps to the doorway, and watches Arizona intently, as he mounts up and rides off past the jut of rock. Sure that he's gone, Grady turns to the men inside the cabin and says, contemptuously, "He calls this loot? It ain't nothin' but chicken feed! The guy's loco! Banks are bulgin' with money and all he wants to do is bankrupt the rail line. You shudda seed the sparkler on that old broad's finger! Worth more'n all these measly twenty-five dollar fines put together. Hell, I gotta mind to go after . . ."

Sage, his demeanor changing, angrily interrupts, "You ain't got a mind, Grady, that's yer trouble. You only been ridin' with us 'bout four months now, but if it weren't fer Arizona, you'd be cleanin' out spittoons or figgerin' how to bust outta some old jailhouse. I knowed that 'cause he only took ya when Gyp's brother in Kansas City done asked him to help git yer sorry self outta some fix. Mebbe it ain't a fortune, but I ain't had to worry 'bout my next meal or lodgings all these years, either."

Grady takes three quick steps and grabs hold of Sage's beard. "You're as loco as he is, old man. Proof is, he don't never share in the loot. Nobody knows where he holes up, either. Why is that? One of these days I'll trail him and find out."

Sage pushes Grady's hand away. "It ain't gold he's after, donkey head—it's the Curtain Rail Lines owners." Sage pauses and takes a long look at Grady before he continues. "Ah fergit it, you wouldn't unnerstand his reasons anyways."

"I shoulda took that ring, Sage. He gets in my way one more time and I'll . . ." Grady puts his hand on his holstered gun and gets a mean look on his face.

Chapter 3

The railroad passes through Whistle Stop, a busy, small cattle town that had a gold rush boom back in the 1850s, which mostly died out when practically no one found gold. The saloon is attached to the hotel. There are a few other barrooms on Main Street, along with the sheriff's office, a bank, a telegraph office, a doctor's office, a small church with a bell tower, a blacksmith's barn and corral, a dry goods store, and various other stores. Beyond them there are rows of houses lining a few streets, laid out with no special plan.

Arizona Adams rides slowly into town with the afternoon sun behind him, as the church bell rings five times. He tips his hat to some ladies, who smile back at him, before pulling up in front of a building with a sign on its window:

THE WHISTLE STOP GAZETTE
Publisher and Editor
James Courtney, Jr.

In the doorway of the newspaper office stands a beautiful, dark-haired woman in her twenties, wearing denims and a man's blue work shirt. The pencil stuck in her hair is a sure sign that she works at the newspaper. A wide smile comes to her face as she greets the handsome rider. "Beautiful day for a ride, stranger. You from around these parts?"

He dismounts and looks her over slowly, shaking his head as he does. "If you look that good in men's clothes, lady, think what you'd look like in a dress. As it is, guys would think you're just one of the boys . . . if you weren't so . . ."

Defensively, she says, "So what?"

He gets all bashful and tongue-tied. "Well . . . you know what I mean." He takes a quick look around the street to see if anyone is watching, before he grabs her and pushes her in front of him into the newspaper office. Once inside, he kisses her passionately, long and hard. She kisses him back and they both get heated up. When their lips part, the woman looks at him, surprised. "My, my, and what brought that on? Did you miss me?"

With a slow smile, he says, "Well, didn't you miss me?"

She gives him a bemused look. "You want to know if I missed you? Well, Jim, I'm actually really glad you take your mysterious rides, though I think you should tell me where you go . . . in case I need you. But then I say to myself that you work too darn hard, and you need to get away once in a while by yourself to relax and think of other things. Any man like you needs that. So, when you're gone, that's when I get things done around here. Why on earth should I miss you?" She's obviously pleased with her reasoning.

As Jim feigns hurt feelings, the office door opens and a middle-aged man and woman, with a boy and girl about eleven and thirteen years old, come in. They are simple but proud farm people. The man takes off his hat.

Jim smiles. "Howdy."

The farmer nods and picks up a copy of the *Whistle Stop Gazette*.

Jim looks them over for a minute, then asks, "Are you the new folks that just took the farm at Well's Corner?"

Looking up from the paper the farmer shows a flicker of surprise. "Why, that's right."

Jim puts his hand out to the man. "Mighty glad to know you. This is my assistant, Ellen Williams. I'm Jim Courtney, the editor and publisher."

"A pleasure to meet you, Miss Williams and Mr. Courtney."

"Call us Ellen and Jim, please." Jim smiles.

Shy about Jim's attention, the man says, "I'm Matt Tracy and this is my wife, Myra. Them two are Marion and Billy. Now we've met up, we'll not take up yer val'able time." He puts the paper down.

Ellen jumps in and says, "Oh, no, please help yourself to the paper. In fact, would you like to subscribe to the *Gazette*?"

"Surely would, Miss Ellen, but y'see," he hesitates, "we're plumb runnin' down on ready cash. What with buyin' the farm and," he holds up the paper, "lookin' fer a hired hand."

Ellen responds warmly, "Well, wouldn't be right for you to miss out on the latest happenings, Matt. And Marion and Billy gotta keep up with the funnies. So, maybe we can strike a deal here. Suppose we offered you a year's subscription to the *Gazette* and, for now, you trade us off a sack of potatoes and a couple of slabs of salty pork? When you have the farm money stuffed in the bank you can pay us for the back issues. How's that, Matt?"

"Right nice of you folks. Sounds fine. C'mon Myra. C'mon kids. We all got chores to do. Bye, folks." Matt tips his hat and they exit happily.

Jim and Ellen smile after them, then she looks at him sheepishly. "Oh my God, Jim, I almost forgot." She rummages through the papers on her desk and fishes out an envelope that she hands to him.

Jim examines the envelope. "That's funny, it's from a law firm in Manhattan, Beagle & Cratchit, Esquires." He opens it.

"Oh, Jim, are you wanted for some terrible crime back East?"

Jim stiffens, always apprehensive about leading his double life as Arizona Adams.

Not understanding his concern, Ellen says, "Relax, I was only joking."

Covering his wariness, he smiles, and says, "Me too, darlin'." As he silently reads the letter, his lips begin to move, and a look of shock and disbelief comes over his face.

"Don't tell me you really are a wanted criminal!"

Jim hands the letter to her. "Here, Ellen, read it for yourself. Aloud, please!"

As she reads aloud, her expression begins to match Jim's, and her voice keeps rising to a crescendo of disbelief.

May 10, 1902

Dear James Courtney: This is to inform you that Mr. Joseph Curtain, owner of the Curtain Rail Lines, died one month ago following a stroke. Mr. Curtain spent the last few years directing an exhaustive search for his sister, June. She was quite young when their parents were killed in an unfortunate accident, and she was sent to be raised by an aunt in Chicago. Much older and already busy making his way in New York, Mr. Curtain lost touch with his sister and the aunt that he never knew himself. During his search he came to know that June had married, settled in Whistle Stop, Arizona, had a son, and had passed away. Mr. Curtain wished to see that the young man inherited the ownership of the Curtain Rail Lines since he had never had children of his own. It was not until shortly before he died that a wire from a detective on the case convinced him that you, Mr. Courtney, are that heir. We, therefore, request that, at your earliest con-

venience, you come to our office in New York City, bringing with you adequate proof of your identity, including any photographs you may have with your mother and your birth certificate, to claim your inheritance.

Ellen looks up at Jim and says, "It's signed 'Mr. Beagle, Beagle & Cratchit, Esquires'." Shocked and completely confused, Ellen and Jim stare wordlessly at one another. Then in a small voice, almost a whisper, Ellen realizes the awesome truth. "Jim, am I awake or what? Do you see what this means? If this *is* real, Arizona Adams has actually been robbing *you* all these years!"

Already knowing this to be the ironic truth, Jim feigns complete shock. "What? What are you saying? Oh my God, Ellen, you're right!"

Now her quick reporter's mind begins to consider the facts. "But why didn't you know your mother was kin to Curtain? I just can't figure that. And I'm just realizing, too, that we've never talked about any of your kin folks. What other secrets do you have?"

He gives her a bothered look. "There are no secrets . . . about my kin. I've never talked about them, because, well, what I know is very sketchy, darlin'. You need to remember, after losing our ranch to the Curtain Rail Lines, my dad died suddenly, and mom passed just a few months later. I always thought it was because her heart was broken."

Ellen gets a very worried look, as if she's holding something back. "That darn railroad is woven into our lives like a big old quilt. Because Jim . . . well, my parents have always talked about how sad that time was for you."

Jim controls his long held anger at the Curtain Rail Lines. "Everything about losing the ranch and then my parents was hard. It cut me so deeply that I never got to ask them about our family history, and plenty of other things I very much wanted to know." He paces then looks at her sadly. "I still miss them so much, Ellen, and sure wish that the three of you had known each other."

"And I'd have given anything to know them, Jim, though I can remember them from the Whistle Stop County Fair when I was a young girl, especially your mom. She had the best cakes and pies and was always so kind and friendly to everyone."

He looks at her with deep love, and then tries to recall all he can about his parents. "But this lawyer's letter makes some sense, because my mom's name was June. And I also know they met in Chicago in 1877, when dad was there at a cattle auction. You know my dad grew up on his parents' ranch here, but mom had been raised in Chicago by her Aunt Flo Green, who was the only kin she ever talked about. But now that I'm thinking on it, mom once did say that her real parents had died in an accident in New York City when she was young. She never mentioned having a brother. But after she passed . . . I found old photographs of her in dad's desk, along with a bunch of other papers, including my birth certificate." Knowing that her questions about that would be next, he says with a wry smile, "And by the way, it said 'Father: James Courtney, Sr., Mother: June Green Courtney'."

"Ah ha! So your mom took your Aunt Flo's name. What about the photographs?"

Amused by her sleuthing, he says, "You sure are a born newspaper woman. So, in one photograph she looked to be maybe eight or ten, with folks I assumed to be her parents and another man, about twenty. There was nothing written on it, and I had no one to ask about the details. That's why my mom's family history and where I came from have always been a mystery for me."

Just then, the front door swings open. An excited man sticks his head in. "Hey, Jim, I just come from the telegraph office. The word came over the wire, they done it again! Arizona Adams and his gang stuck up a Curtain train early this morning. I believe that's the fourth time this year!" And the man ducks out.

Ellen says, "Oh, no, Jim, this is all too unbelievable!"

Jim—absorbing this remarkable turn of events—makes a strong effort to pull himself together, as he walks to the door of the printing room and calls to the old pressman working at the ancient Kluge. "Charley, dust off that type we have standing from the last three train raids this year by the Adams Gang. Just change the date to today and we'll run it on the front page next to the corset ad."

Turning to Ellen, he says, "I made up my mind. I can't go to New York."

"You're not going? How can you possibly mean that? Don't you want to finally solve this mystery?"

Jim smiles, slowly. "Well, who's going to run the paper while I'm gone, Ellen?"

Indignant, she gently smacks his arm. "You just pack your bags and get going, Jim Courtney, before we both wake up from this dream. Go now and claim your birthright, before the Curtain Rail Lines goes bust!"

Jim gives Ellen a quick kiss and exits the newspaper office on a half run, chuckling to himself, "My clever sweetheart has no idea how deep this mystery runs."

Chapter 4

Gathered on the platform of the Whistle Stop railroad station is a small crowd of folks, waiting for the train heading east to Kansas City, Chicago, and New York. Among them is Jim, looking handsome as ever, wearing his big white hat, dressed in a tan Western suit, with an old suitcase by his side. He is looking at Ellen with a lot of love showing on his face.

Nervous and concerned, she says, "Did you bring the proof of your identity?"

"Don't worry darlin', I have everything I need."

"I'm sure you do, Jim. But more importantly, I want you to watch yourself."

"Watch myself?"

"Well, New York is full of card sharks, con men, fast women, and Lord knows what else! Those people can take advantage."

He laughs. "Don't worry, honey, I fought in the Spanish American War.

Now she laughs, "Sure, as a correspondent."

He smiles along with her. "You always forget that I did my army training first. So, you can be sure that I can take care of myself." As the train comes down the track and lurches to a stop, with clouds of steam erupting, Jim embraces and kisses Ellen. "Now you're in charge, so I'm counting on you." Hating to leave her, but looking forward to what this trip will hold for him, he climbs aboard.

Ellen waves after him, "Good luck. Telegraph me with news. And . . . I'll be missing you, every minute."

He flashes her a big smile. Once in the car, he takes a seat and waves to Ellen out of the window. She continues to wave back until the train has pulled out of the station. The conductor who was on the westbound train that the Arizona Adams Gang robbed just a few days ago is coming down the aisle, collecting tickets. He approaches Jim, who fishes his ticket out of his pocket and hands it to the conductor. The conductor gives him a good, hard look. "Say, you sure look familiar."

"I should, good sir. And maybe someday I won't have to be paying for a ticket."

Now the conductor is totally puzzled. "How so, mister?"

Jim, knowing exactly what the man senses, and respecting him for being cool during the train robbery, takes pleasure in saying, "Well, my uncle is Joseph Curtain."

The conductor jumps in, thinking Jim is joking. "Well, now, old Joe Curtain's your uncle? That's so nice. Means you can play with your trains any time you've a mind to."

He looks up at the conductor. "Sorry, I didn't mean to brag. It's just that in my uncle's will he . . ."

The conductor jumps in again. "He gave you the railroad, right? Any uncle worth his salt would do the same. Tell you what, when you're in Manhattan why don't you just amble on over to the Hippodrome Theater. Just tell 'em you're a friend of mine, Henry Parnell, and they'll let you in free. You see, I own that theater." The conductor chuckles at his joke, gives Jim another hard look, punches his ticket, and goes on down the aisle. He whispers something to another conductor, as they both glance at Jim.

Jim smiles to himself, pulls his hat down over his face, and gets some sleep. Over the next few days, he takes his meals in the dining car and enjoys the scene out the window, passing through the great states of Missouri, Illinois, Indiana, Ohio, and Pennsylvania, while speeding toward New York City. Mostly he keeps to himself, thinks about Ellen, the Arizona Adams Gang, and what he'll need to do to deal with the gang once he owns the Curtain Rail Lines.

Henry Parnell, conductor and 'theater owner', calls out "Next stop, Exchange Place, Jersey City, New Jersey—get the ferry to New York City." Jim stirs from his sleep as the train pulls into the terminal. He gets up, takes his old suitcase, and prepares to leave the train. As Jim steps out onto the platform, Henry Parnell and the other conductor lean out the window, waving goodbye. "Goodbye, sir. Don't you worry, we'll take good care of your train for you!" The second conductor mocks, "Yeah, boss, don't worry about Arizona Adams!" At the mention of the outlaw, Henry Parnell gives Jim another very hard look.

Jim tips his hat, saying, "You can be sure I won't be worrying about him, boys," and chuckles to himself as he lines up with the other passengers to get the waiting ferry. His anticipation grows as he takes in the awesome New York City skyline, while crossing the mighty Hudson River. After making his way through the bustling ferry terminal and out to the street, he is immediately confronted by the hurrying crowds, jostled by gentlemen in top hats brushing past him, and rebuffed brusquely by a proper woman in a stylish Edwardian dress and bonnet, when he tries to ask her for directions. Finally, a cop steers him toward 59th Street and Fifth Avenue, where Beagle & Cratchit have their offices. Jim says "Much obliged," and starts out, carrying his suitcase.

The cop calls after him, "Hey cowboy, that's way more than a mile off."

He keeps walking, so glad to be taking in the sights of this great city. Well more than an hour later, Jim walks along Central Park South toward Fifth Avenue. Seeing the horse carriages parked in front of The Park Hotel, he fishes in his pocket for a sugar cube, which he feeds to an emaciated-looking horse. "Good girl." Petting the horse's nose, he sees the driver is sleeping, shakes his head, and continues up the street, unaware that the horse, pulling its carriage, is walking right behind him, seeking more sugar. The horse hungrily nuzzles Jim's coat pocket. A look of sudden apprehension crosses his face, as he recalls Ellen's warnings about the evils of the Big City. Jim draws his six-gun and whirls, poking the gun barrel right into the startled horse's muzzle. Passersby panic and duck for cover. The real situation dawns on Jim, and he ruefully returns his gun to its holster, but not before a policeman who witnessed Jim's actions hurries up to him.

"Stop right there. I seen you pull that gun on this poor horse!"

Jim talks easy. "No, no, my good man! I thought the horse was, well, a pickpocket. You see, my girl in Arizona warned me about . . ." He looks around at the gathering crowd. The carriage driver, now awake, jumps out of his carriage and rushes over to them.

The cop scratches his head, "Well, if that don't beat all! I never heard of a horse that was a pickpocket!"

The carriage driver pipes in, saying, "Jennie ain't no pickpocket! I've knowed her since she was a little filly. You wouldn't ever want to know a nicer horse."

Jim protests. "You got it wrong, partner, of course the horse is innocent. I only meant . . ."

Angry, the cop has heard enough. "Hand over that gun, buddy. You cowboys are all trigger happy."

Jim hesitates but hands the gun over to him. The cop rolls the cylinder, empties out all the bullets, and hands Jim the gun. "I got to get back on me beat and the horse ain't gonna bring no charges. So get along with you now, and don't hang out here." He says to the crowd, "We got dancin' bears and roller skatin' chimps, but I never heard of no pickpocketin' horses! All right, it's all over, break it up, move along now!" The crowd breaks up as the cop walks away, pocketing Jim's bullets and muttering to himself, "That dude wants me to believe that the horse was picking his pocket! He shudda stayed on the ranch!"

Jim laughs and walks across the street to a ten-story grey, stone building and enters. Inside, he opens a door bearing the gold-lettered names Beagle & Cratchit, Esquires, on the pebbled glass. Putting down his suitcase and taking off his cowboy hat, he announces himself to the receptionist, "Howdy there, I'm James Courtney to see Mr. Beagle."

The pretty young woman looks up, a bit surprised to see the big, handsome man in Western gear standing before her. "Oh, Mr. Courtney, why we've been expecting you. Come right this way." She flashes him a big smile as she ushers him into a spacious office with mahogany panels and a fine oriental rug. "Mr. Beagle, Mr. Courtney has finally arrived."

At the far end of the large room is a huge mahogany desk. "Ah, come in, Mr. Courtney." Jim hears a voice but sees no one. Then the big, leather chair at the desk whirls around, and Jim sees a tiny man seated behind the desk. He is a sharp-featured, elderly man, well tailored, wearing gold-rimmed glasses. Rising, he puts out his hand and talks fast. "Have a seat. Have a cigar? Have a good trip? I'm Mr. Beagle."

Jim walks over to Beagle and shakes his hand cordially. "Pleased to meet you, Mr. Beagle."

Beagle waves him to a chair opposite himself. "Before we get to the business at hand, I want to tell you that Mr. Beamish has reserved a suite for you at The Park Hotel, across the street, all expenses paid."

"Mr. Beamish? The Park Hotel, you say?" Jim smiles.

"That's right. Mr. Beamish also invited you to attend the Board of Directors' meeting of the Curtain Rail Lines at 1450 Broadway, that's at Forty-first Street, at 2 P.M. tomorrow. He's the current chairman of the board. Now, let's get down to business. First, did you bring proof of your identity?"

Sitting down, a bit amazed by Beagle, he looks through his bag. Pulling out a folder, he flips through it. "Brought my birth certificate, old pictures of me with my parents, and a picture of my mother as a young girl with folks I believe to be her family. There's also some current bills with my address, letters, and my army discharge papers."

Beagle looks over at the folder. "Fine, very thorough. May I see them?"

Jim hands his folder to Beagle, who then reaches into his desk and pulls out Joseph Curtain's folder. Jim sees him take out the identical photograph of his mom, with the folks he believes are her parents, and the young man, only this photograph has writing on it. Beagle compares it to the picture in Jim's folder. Then he inspects the photographs of Jim with his parents and the other documents very carefully. He looks up at Jim, who is craning his neck to see the writing on Curtain's matching photograph.

"Is there a problem, Mr. Courtney?"

"No problem, Mr. Beagle, it's just that I don't know my grandparents' names or how they passed. It would mean a lot to me to fill in those facts."

Beagle hands him Curtain's matching photograph with the words "Mother, Dad, June and myself in 1865" written on it. Jim stares at it while Beagle delivers his verdict. "Well, as you can see, there's no doubt about it, your mom was Curtain's sister, June. Your grandfather was Joseph Curtain, Sr., a businessman. Your grandmother was Beatrice Green Curtain. As I heard it, they were riding in an open coach when an old tree branch broke off and landed on them. Both were killed instantly. The only relative was your grandmother's sister Flo Green in Chicago, so that's where your mother was sent."

"Thank you kindly, Mr. Beagle." Jim looks at him expectantly.

"And your papers are all ship shape. You know, Mr. Courtney, you can't be too careful with the law, which is a kind of mixed up hodge-podge. At any rate, as far as I'm concerned, you *are* Mr. James Courtney, Mr. Curtain's nephew."

Jim is pleased. "Then since I *am* me, I must be the new owner of the Curtain Rail Lines, right?"

Hesitantly, Beagle looks at him very seriously. "Well . . . let's say that as of now you are the heir apparent. But no, you are not the owner. Not yet. You see, Mr. Courtney, Mr. Curtain insisted on an important proviso."

Now Jim is puzzled. "A proviso?"

Beagle opens another drawer of his desk, and looks intently at the papers he brings out. "Let me read this to you. This is an excerpt from Mr. Curtain's Last Will and Testament." He reads:

> *James Courtney, now residing in Whistle Stop, Arizona—subject to proof of his identity as my late sister June's son, and that his character and reputation are above reproach, with no instances of law breaking activities, no matter how small—is named as my sole heir. I wish him to inherit my controlling shares of the Curtain Rail Lines Corporation, with this proviso: Since the company's trains have been subjected to repeated robberies by an outlaw gang in the Arizona Territory, and since these robberies could bankrupt the Curtain Rail Lines Corporation unless they are stopped—which I wouldn't wish upon my nephew—it is therefore my wish that James Courtney shall inherit the aforesaid controlling shares if, and only if, he captures or kills the leader of the outlaw gang robbing the trains, who is*

*known as Arizona Adams. This is a crucial task that
I have not been able to accomplish during my life-
time. There can be no exception to this proviso.*

Beagle takes off his glasses and looks up at Jim.

Jim is sitting rigidly upright, staring at Beagle. In a very as-tonished voice, he says, "Only if I capture or kill Arizona Adams?"

Still all business, but noting his reaction, Beagle responds, "Certainly an unusual proviso, but Mr. Curtain was very much in earnest and in his right mind when he made it, and Mr. Beamish and the other board members accepted the proviso and backed him up. So that's it, Mr. Courtney."

Now comprehending the full meaning of the will, Jim rises slowly, lost in thought. Mr. Beagle takes his arm and guides him to the door, then takes hold of Jim's limp hand warmly and shakes it. "Best of luck to you, Mr. Courtney. Let us know as soon as you have fulfilled Mr. Curtain's proviso—and happy hunting!"

Jim exits past the receptionist, deep in thought about his un-cle's proviso. She waves but he doesn't notice. He leaves the building and walks across the street to The Park Hotel in a daze.

The Park Hotel lobby is finely appointed with thick rugs, gold-framed pictures, and settees covered in plush, scarlet fabric. At the desk he identifies himself to the reservations clerk and a bellhop. The bellhop notices Jim's Western garb and boots with interest, picks up his old suitcase and ushers him to the elevator. Emerging on the top floor, they enter a palatial suite. Jim looks around, say-ing, "But where's *my* room?"

The bellhop is puzzled. "You're in it, sir."

Jim is a bit amazed by the place. There's a large sitting area, with two plush sofas, club chairs and a coffee table, a king sized bed at the far end of the vast room, and beautifully draped win-dows that look out on Central Park. "This whole place is for *me*?"

"Yes, sir. Will you require room service?"

"What I'll require is a map."

Not getting the joke. "Sir?"

"Forget it. Just tell me, where's the nearest bar?"

He understands Jim's need. "Yes sir, that's the Splendide, just across the street." He puts out his hand for a tip. Jim, thinking he wants to shake hands, grasps his hand and shakes it. The bellhop lets go and looks right into Jim's eyes until he comprehends.

"Oh, right. I get it." He reaches into his pocket, finds two bits, and hands over the tip.

The bellhop taps his hat. "Thank you," then exits.

Jim looks in the mirror. He draws his empty gun, aims at himself, and pulls the trigger. Click. Shaking his head in disbelief, he says out loud, "You're dead, Arizona Adams."

Chapter 5

Later that night, dressed in his Western suit and cowboy hat, Jim exits The Park Hotel, crosses the street, and enters the Cafe Splendide. As he sits at the bar, he comes to the attention of a brassy blonde, obviously a prostitute, working the cafe's patrons. She takes the bar stool next to Jim. Seductively, she says, "Hi, honey. Like a little company?"

Not really wanting her company, he barely nods at her.

She looks him over. "Where you from, honey?"

He's still reluctant. "Arizona."

Making a big deal, she says, "Well, why don't you and me drink a little toast to Arizona?"

Now trapped, he turns to look at her. "Well, uh . . . well, okay."

The prostitute calls to the bartender, "Scotch, Vernon."

Vernon winks surreptitiously at the prostitute. "Sorry, ma'am, we're not allowed to serve drinks to ladies at the bar. Maybe you and the gentleman would prefer to be seated in our restaurant area. We'd be very glad to serve you there."

"That all right with you, hon? It's the law, y'know."

"Sure. Okay."

"Hey Vernon, bring us a bottle of Killarney Scotch and ice." She smiles and Jim follows her to a small table in the adjoining restaurant, where he helps her to her seat and sits across from her. She looks into his eyes. "Why, you Western boys sure know how to treat a lady."

Vernon brings the bottle of Scotch and two glasses. The prostitute fills Jim's glass to the brim, and pours only a tiny bit into her own glass. She lifts her glass to him. "What's your name, hon?"

He raises his glass to her. "Jim." He takes a sip.

She sips and looks him over. "Nice manly name. Suits you. I'm very sensitive, Jim. I catch things, feelings, y'know. And I got a feelin' there's somethin' bothering you. Have another Scotch?"

"No thanks. What's *your* name?"

"Gladys, but they all call me Glad around here 'cause I'm always happy. Hey, why you drinkin' so slow. Drink up, Arizona."

Surprised by that, he looks around to see if anyone heard her, then gives her a strong look and drinks. She pours more in his glass, obviously trying to get Jim drunk. She flashes her eyes at him and he reluctantly downs the drink. "Sorry, Glad. I'm not much of a drinker."

"Help you drown your troubles, Arizona. In fact, what is your problem? Tell it to Glad. Two heads, y'know." She flashes a big smile, and then she fills his glass again.

He takes a sip. Glad is succeeding in making Jim drunk. His words are now a bit slurred, as his eyes stay fixed on his glass. "Well, s'pose you had to capture or kill yourself. Not that that's my problem, you understand." He glances up at her to see if she's following the story, takes a sip, then asks her, "But just out of curiosity, how would you do that?"

Thinking he's joking, she plays along. "Well, I'd hide in an alley and then when I saw myself walking by, I'd take out a gun, jump out and kill myself. Simple!"

Very drunk now, he takes out his gun with no bullets in it. Her eyes widen, as she does not know it is empty. "Aw, this is too much of a problem." He looks at the gun, then puts it away. "I tell you, Glad, I feel like saying the hell with the whole proviso."

The prostitute suddenly becomes frightened, realizing that Jim is serious. "'Scuse me, honey, gotta see a man about a dog. Be right back and then we'll find out how you can capture or kill yourself." She leaves, wending her way through the barroom crowd to the hefty bouncer at the far end of the bar. Through a drunken haze, Jim sees her wave at him with a phony smile. She says something urgently to the bouncer. The bouncer eyes Jim and then approaches him cautiously.

With false geniality, he says, "Glad tells me you got a problem—uh, how to capture or kill yourself?"

Now very drunk, he replies, "Yup. They won't give me what belongs to me unless I kill myself . . . or capture myself. You see, it's a l'il hard to unnerstand, I know."

The bouncer sizes him up. "Well, it sounds like you *really* do have a problem, which requires a clear head to solve it. Whadda ya say we go outside 'n just clear our heads in the nice fresh air so's we can deal with this here problem of yours."

"Ex'lent idea."

The bouncer helps Jim from his chair. Jim throws some money on the table and stumbles along with the bouncer through the kitchen to the back door. The bouncer opens the door and stands courteously aside. "You first, sir."

Jim lurches out. The bouncer quickly slams the door shut behind him. Jim finds himself alone in the alley next to the Cafe Splendide. Bumping against some garbage cans, he stumbles across the street to The Park Hotel. He weaves his way into his suite, crashes on the bed fully clothed, and instantly falls asleep.

Chapter 6

Jim is hung-over as he steps off of the elevator and enters the reception area of the posh offices of the Curtain Rail Lines. Dressed in his best Western suit, he takes a look around, removes his hat, and shakes his head like an untamed stallion, to clear the cobwebs. The receptionist looks up, immediately taken by the handsome Westerner before her. With a big smile, he says, "Howdy, ma'am, Mr. Courtney to see Mr. Beamish."

Realizing who he is, she smiles right back at him. "Oh yes, Mr. Courtney. I'm Miss Eaton. Mr. Beamish is expecting you. Please follow me." She leads the way through a beautiful carved door.

As Jim follows her down the immaculate corridor, he feels like he's touring a royal palace. The walls are covered with damask wallpaper and lined with gold-framed, original art by European painters. They stop in front of a door with a gleaming plaque, designating it as the Curtain Rail Lines conference room. Miss Eaton opens the door and leads him to a seat at the end of the long conference table. After taking one last, appreciative glance at him, she leaves.

The meeting of the Board of Directors is just starting. Jim notes that there are a dozen Directors present. Most of them are middle-aged and conservatively dressed. At the head of the table is

Albert Beamish, a paunchy, well-dressed man with an extremely self-important manner, about fifty years old, nods at Jim and continues to speak pompously. "Then are we agreed, gentlemen, that all members of the Curtain Rail Lines Board of Directors will receive a fifteen percent pay raise, to begin first of next month, which will be retroactive to February 25th of last year? All in favor of this . . ."

He barely has the words out of his mouth when all of the Directors raise their hands high in the air, yelling "Aye!"

Beamish is very gratified. "The Ayes have it."

Jim is immediately puzzled, since the company is supposed to be in bad financial shape—certainly with some thanks to the activities of his Arizona Adams Gang. Seeing Jim's consternation over this proposal, Beamish's genial mood changes. "Of course, gentlemen, as you know, some of the stockholders are calling for an accounting. But even though there's no doubt that we deserve a raise for all of the hard work we do to develop and secure new business for the corporation, I would suggest that you refrain from discussing the proposed increase openly at this time."

Dilbert Finley, a chubby man in his early forties, calls out in a sycophantic tone, "Right! You're absolutely right about that, Mr. Beamish!"

Noting that Jim, at the foot of the table, is still looking mighty puzzled, Beamish says, "Before we get to the main company business and, most importantly, our finances, I have been called upon to announce the forthcoming marriage of Billy, here, to Miss Renee DeVain. Most of you know the fortunate lady. She's that very cute cigarette girl at the Hallelujah Club." Billy is smiling like the cat that ate the canary. He is about seventy-five years old, and lifts his walking cane to salute his associates. "Don't forget, Billy has invited us to meet his young bride-to-be at a prenuptial affair tomorrow evening at 8 o'clock in the dining salon of the *Hotel Des Jardins.*"

Beamish looks toward the opening door and all heads turn as a beautiful, stylishly dressed woman in her early thirties enters. She takes a seat near Jim, who notices that there is an air of *hauteur* and wealth about her. Beamish nods to her and smiles in an extremely cordial manner. She smiles and nods in return. Some of the others acknowledge her as well. Now very curious, Jim thinks, "Wow, who is she, and what's she doing here?"

Beamish changes his expression to serious concern. "Now, back to business. Unfortunately, our overall financial condition has worsened once again." He turns to some graphs placed on a tripod beside him and turns the placards one by one. Each graph, successively, shows lines plunging downward. "I'm afraid, gentlemen, that the public is becoming reluctant to ride our trains that pass through the Arizona Territory. These graphs show that shipments, too, through Arizona to the far west are down by almost fifty percent. Our reputation for passenger security is under fire, and the insurance companies are about to cancel our policies. We have to do something effective because there are some stockholders threatening to call a special meeting to elect a new Board of Directors."

The Directors register their deep concern. There is general commotion.

"Order, order, gentlemen, I'm afraid that the word is spreading—'Don't ride with the Curtain Rail Lines and don't ship with them either, especially through Arizona.' We're afraid that copycat gangs are going to spring up in other states due to the success of the Arizona Adams Gang. Since our inter-city tonnage in the Western states and territories has dropped from sixty-five percent to twenty-five percent, we've been forced to close some depots and stations in small towns on those routes. Put it all together and it could spell bankruptcy. If we could stop that son-of-a-gun Arizona Adams and his gang it would go a long way toward solving this problem."

Jim thinks to himself, "Well boys, bankruptcy was my greatest desire for you all." He listens carefully as various Directors comment about the gang.

"Those damn outlaws!"

"We have to get the scoundrels."

"They didn't work a day for those contracts."

Beamish looks around. "Yes, we have to get them, but we've already tried everything! Posses led by the sheriff in Whistle Stop have failed—those idiots couldn't catch a cold at 120 below at the North Pole. The armed guards we put on some of the trains drank themselves into a stupor and slept right through the raids. We put undercover operatives in Whistle Stop and other nearby towns to get information about the Arizona Adams Gang. They spent their time in the local barrooms, padded their expense accounts, and some of them ran off with the dance hall girls. Nothing has worked!" Grimly, he says, "Gentlemen, we only have one last card to play."

From around the table the various Directors yell out.

"What's that?"

"What are you getting at?"

"Spell it out, Beamish."

Beamish spreads his hands and gestures to the table. "Gentlemen, I'm afraid the only way to stop this outlaw and his gang is for . . . for all of us to go out to Whistle Stop and deal with this Arizona Adams and his gang *ourselves*! A sudden silence falls over the Directors, then a burst of dismayed conversation. Beamish defends his position, proclaiming in a loud voice over the din, "If you want to protect your jobs, your future financial well-being, and your very comfortable way of life, you'll all be with me when we head out to Whistle Stop."

Old Billy yells out, "What about me? I'm not gonna spend my honeymoon dodging bullets in Arizona."

Beamish calms him. "Everybody but you Billy and George Cavendish. But the rest of the board has to be there so we can make quick decisions based on first-hand knowledge. George Cavendish will be in charge here and continue to run the day-to-day operations while we're gone. Also, men, I know that this is the right way to finally deal with Arizona Adams, because we'll be in the best of hands on this mission."

A few of the board members yell out, "We will?" "Why?"

Beamish milks his presentation. "By a great stroke of good luck, we have among us a man who knows the Arizona Territory like the back of his hand, and—for reasons that will soon become all too clear—I'm sure he'll be more than glad to lead us against Arizona Adams. Here he is, men, I give you Mr. Jim Courtney, a longtime native citizen of Whistle Stop, the nephew of our late, great leader, Mr. Joseph Curtain, and heir apparent to the Curtain Rail Lines, provided that he kills or captures Arizona Adams."

There is dead silence. Every head in the room turns to Jim, who suddenly feels ambushed. Rising very hesitantly, he says, "Well, gentlemen, I'm mighty glad to meet you all, but I hardly think I am qualified to lead you, especially against Arizona Adams."

Beamish cuts in quickly, "Don't be so modest, Mr. Courtney. You have the look of a born leader of men."

Dilbert Finley, the chubby director, calls out in the same sycophantic manner, "You're right, Mr. Beamish. He sure does look like a leader. You're right!"

Beamish nods in approval. "Thanks, Mr. Finley. Then no need to put it to a vote. Congratulations to you, Mr. Courtney. This meeting is now adjourned. Please be prepared to leave for Whistle Stop on Thursday morning at 9 A.M., three days from now. The company will pay transportation costs and all expenses."

As the Directors file out—some nodding to Jim, the others talking animatedly among themselves about their impending trip—

Beamish joins Jim and shakes his hand. "Well now, Mr. Courtney . . . do you mind if I call you Jim? Call me Al, short for Albert. Mr. Beagle told me he informed you of the details of Mr. Curtain's will, including the proviso."

Jim looks Mr. Beamish in the eyes, already recognizing the rattlesnake he's dealing with. "Yessir. But don't you think you kind of railroaded me into this hunt for Arizona Adams?"

Beamish smiles. "Railroaded you? I like that. Be fun travelling with you. But look at it my way, Jim. Since you're required to capture or kill Arizona anyway by the conditions of the proviso, I figured I could be a big help to you. I'll be right there whenever you need anything, and I mean anything! And having the board there, too, will insure immediate Curtain Lines board approvals for any actions you'll need to take to get the job done."

Jim hides his true feelings. "The truth is, what I'm gonna need is luck and lots of it."

Beamish is full of confidence. "Under your leadership, with me as your second-in-command, Jim, this fellow Arizona Adams had better sleep with one eye open."

Jim shoots back, wryly, "Personally, I'll be lucky if I get any sleep at all."

Beamish's attention shifts to the stylish woman who is gathering her things preparing to leave. "Don't worry about that," he says, taking Jim's arm. "I'd like you to meet Nicole. She was Joe Curtain's wife before they got a friendly divorce just over a year ago. She still owns a substantial block of Curtain Rail Lines stock." Nicole looks up, sees them approaching and smiles warmly at Jim. Beamish gives Nicole a meaningful look. "Jim Courtney, I'm pleased to present Nicole Corwin." Then he turns to Jim. "Nicky to us."

Jim's eyes sweep over her beautiful lavender hat with feathers, blonde hair, and matching lavender dress, made of silk and lace.

She is stunning. He gives a partial bow. "I'm very pleased to meet you, ma'am."

She takes in his handsome face and smiles. "And I'm *so* glad to meet you at last, Mr. Courtney. It's such a thrill to be face-to-face with you!"

He is puzzled. "A thrill?"

"Yes, Mr. Courtney. Joseph searched high and low for you. During the last few months of his life it became his passion. Both as his ex-wife and friend, I grew to share it with him. The last detective he hired finally wired him the news of his sister June's married name, that she had already passed quite some time ago, and that you were her only son, just before he had the stroke and died. Meeting you personally would have been the fulfilment of his greatest desire." She squeezes Jim's arm warmly. "So, now that you're here and taking over his beloved rail line, we must get to know one another."

Choosing to be conservative with Nicky and Beamish, he says, "Long way to go, ma'am, before I can take over. Maybe never."

"I admire your courage. Taking on that vicious outlaw and his murderous gang! Aren't you afraid?"

Jim pauses, looking from Nicky to Beamish and back to Nicky. "Well . . . not so much of Arizona Adams as . . ."

Nicky interrupts. "You amaze me. Most men would be quaking with fear. But you're not. If that isn't courage, what is? Why aren't you afraid?"

"Well, ma'am, you might say . . . well . . . it's because I know myself," he says sheepishly.

Nicky says to Beamish, "Isn't he marvelous! No fear! No trembling! I've just got to hear your whole story, Jim. May I call you Jim? But I must go now. I'll be looking forward to seeing you at Billy's engagement party tomorrow evening." She smiles at Jim, nods to Beamish and exits. Her perfume lingers.

Both men watch her go, appreciating her luminous beauty. Beamish turns to Jim. "Are you comfortable at The Park Hotel? Can I do anything for you?"

Jim looks Beamish over, already knowing that handling him over the weeks ahead will be a tough challenge. "Thanks a lot. I'm good."

Beamish holds out his hand and they shake. "Excellent, I'll see you tomorrow night, Jim. And don't worry, we'll get Arizona."

Jim lets go of Beamish's hand. "Perhaps."

Chapter 7

Outside the *Hotel des Jardins*, fashionable coaches, Hansom cabs, and an occasional gasoline-powered Cadillac or Oldsmobile Curved Runabout drive up and discharge stylish men and women dressed in evening clothes. A uniformed doorman opens the doors to the coaches. Jim and Beamish step out of one and enter the hotel. Shortly afterward, Nicky's ornate private carriage arrives. The doorman extends his hand, welcomes her and says, "Good evening, Miss Corwin." She smiles and enters the hotel swathed in fur, looking exquisite.

As Nicky joins Beamish and Jim in the dining salon, their eyes light with pleasure at the sight of her. The *maitre'd* shepherds them to a table, as heads turn to appreciate Nicky's beauty. The other Curtain Rail Lines Directors and their wives are already there. They are paying their respects to old Billy and his young, simpering *fiancée*, Renee DeVain.

Already uncomfortable in his evening clothes, Jim makes note of the Directors and their wives and girlfriends, like any good newspaper editor. Seeing each of the men in this posh place, dressed in impeccable evening attire, with their bejeweled women, he concludes that returning to Whistle Stop with them to capture Arizona Adams will prove to be a booby-trapped battleground for him, unless he can think of a clever plan—and right quickly.

George Cavendish stands and raises his glass to Billy. Jim notes that he has a walrus moustache, high-parted haircut, and horn-rimmed glasses, just like President Theodore Roosevelt. Cavendish says, "A toast to Renee and Billy—may your fires burn forever, and may you never run out of cigarettes."

Jim laughs to himself because, aside from Cavendish's appearance, he clearly has no other traits in common with the president. Then another director, Felix Herkimer, who appears to be in his late forties, rises and says with drunken mirth, "Here, here, George!" He offers his toast to Billy and Renee, followed by toasts from several other equally inebriated directors. While watching the proceedings, Jim is a bit surprised when Nicky briefly takes his hand and squeezes it warmly. Beamish notices her flirtatious move and his eyes narrow.

The orchestra begins to play and some couples take to the dance floor. Beamish, barely hiding a mocking smile, asks Jim, "What sort of dancing do they do in Whistle Stop? Hoedown, barn dances?"

Jim takes a gander at Beamish's smug stare, then looks at Nicky questioningly. She takes his hand and they join the couples on the dance floor. Beamish watches, smiling, until he sees that Jim is a very good dancer. He sits unhappily alone until Jim and Nicky return to the table. Resuming his false geniality, he snaps his fingers in the air, calling out *"Gerson!"* The waiter frowns at his mispronunciation of *garçon,* as he comes to their table.

"What'll it be, Nicky? The *poulet de fragond* is the *piece-de-resistance* here."

"Then I'll have that, Albert."

Beamish watches Jim study the menu. "And you, Jim? Oh, I'm sorry, the menu is in French. If you have difficulty with the language, just ask me."

Not taking his eyes off the menu, Jim orders. "Let's see, *Je aiment avoir le boeuf cuis à l'étouffée, les pommes de terre* et *l'asperge. Et après le dîner, du café. Et pour le dessert Sherbet Romanoff, s'il vous plait. Merci.*" Jim looks at the waiter and nods, as Beamish sits slack-jawed, astonished that Jim can speak French. "Thanks for the kind offer, Al, but after fighting in the Spanish American War . . ."

Beamish interrupts, asking doubtfully, "You were a Rough Rider, with the president?"

Seeing that Beamish is incredulous, Jim enjoys recounting the facts. "A Rough Rider? Not exactly. I was in Cuba and saw some action, but early on the army made me a reporter. That's how I came to spend a couple of months in the Paris offices of the *New York Herald Tribune* covering the Treaty of Paris. Learning French was mandatory. When I returned home, I founded the *Whistle Stop Gazette. C'est tout!*" Beamish attempts a smile that fails.

Throughout dinner, as the waiter serves courses and removes empty plates, Jim pretty much plays the quiet man, not wanting to reveal too much more about himself. Nicky is happy to smile at him and dance with him between each course. She is obviously taken by Jim's charms. Beamish tries to hide his deepening annoyance at her attraction to him. The moment he finishes his dessert, he says with possessive authority, "Time to call it a night folks. Shall we pay our respects and go, Nicky?"

"You go ahead, Albert. I'll call you tomorrow. Jim and I have some loose ends to discuss. Night."

Beamish is not used to being brushed-off. "Well, yes, until tomorrow." He rises and exits sullenly.

Nicky turns and gives Jim a radiant smile. "I'd like to have a cozy little chat, Jim, if it's alright with you. I think we'll be more comfortable at my place. Besides, I'm just a wee bit tipsy, and I'd appreciate an escort."

Not bargaining for this and thinking of Ellen, he says, "Well, you should know I have a . . ." He stops himself, seeing no point in mentioning Ellen, and instead decides to be a gentleman. "Well sure, Nicky."

*

As Nicky's carriage turns into a private driveway, she gently places her hand on his knee and smiles. The carriage stops in front of her palatial mansion on Gramercy Park. Jim helps Nicky out and they enter the mansion.

In the front hall a maid takes their coats. Nicky says imperiously, "You may leave for the evening, Eugenia. I won't be needing you."

She nods and says, "Thank you, madame," then puts their coats in a closet by the door.

"Come, my friend." Nicky beckons to Jim and leads him up a wide, marble stairway. Following her, he looks around at the opulence, which assures him that the ex-Mrs. Curtain got a big piece of Joe Curtain's money.

They enter a large room, beautifully furnished with authentic Louis XVI chairs and sofas. She stretches out seductively on a chaise lounge. Seeing this, Jim looks about somewhat nervously, and finally settles down in a satin-covered armchair opposite Nicky. She smiles warmly. "Now we can talk in comfort. There's so much I want to know about you."

"There's nothing much to tell."

Nicky coos, "I love strong, silent men."

"I'm just a small town newspaper publisher."

She sits up and looks into his eyes. "Not any more. You'll soon be the head of a major railroad. You need to know a lot, Jim, and I may be in a good position to help you quite a bit with that. Joe Curtain and I often discussed his problems in running the company. I could do the same for you."

Now he gets her angle. "I'd sure appreciate that."

She flirts on. "I could be your personal assistant."

He turns on the charm. "Well, you are too fine for that sort of work, Nicky."

"I would welcome it, Jim. I am fascinated by the railroad business." Then she smiles and asks, "Would you please excuse me for a moment?" Jim nods as Nicky rises and goes into her adjoining bedroom.

Jim sits stiffly, waiting. He thinks, "Boy, am I in it deep now." She emerges in a few minutes wearing a very revealing and beautiful *négligée*. His eyes widen.

"Jim, in the world of big business you can't trust anyone." She sits on the arm of his chair and puts her face close to his.

He's again intoxicated by her perfume, but he's all business. "I sure know that, Nicky."

Now she stands and walks back and forth before him, the *négligée* hardly concealing her shapely body. "There's something you don't know, Jim."

He can't help staring at her, and asks, "What's that?"

"It's Beamish."

"Beamish?"

She stops before him. "Yes. He's been playing up to me. He thinks that if he and I combine our shares in the company and you get killed by Arizona Adams, then our shares will insure that he can take over the Curtain Rail Lines. However, Jim, if you and I were to combine our shares instead, then he will be in the minority—no matter how many other directors vote their shares with him—and his little plan would be destroyed. You see?"

Jim is not surprised by her scheme and corrects her reasoning. "Gosh, Nicky, as I see it, if I get killed then Beamish's plan will work for him, but if I get Arizona and fulfill the proviso, then I alone will have control of the company. Right?"

Avoiding his question, Nicky becomes extremely seductive. "Darling, I know we've only known each other a short time, but there's something about you that tells me you and I are star-crossed, that we were made for each other." She touches his arm, then backs away from him toward the bedroom. "Please get comfortable, Jim darling. Relax before we explore the possibilities for our future. I know that once we spend the night together, you'll come around to seeing things my way."

Jim is confused. "Explore what? Spend the night together?"

Nicky stares at him, unbelievingly.

Jim suddenly comprehends her meaning and says, "Sure, sure. I guess you might say that we may be star-crossed . . . because, after all, technically, you are my ex-aunt."

"What does that have to do with now, my darling?"

Seeing that this obvious fact means nothing to her, he says, "And then there's Ellen . . ."

This gets a quick response. "And who, may I ask, is Ellen?"

"My *fiancée*."

Nicky's eyes suddenly grow cold and hard. "I see." She closes her *négligée,* openly showing her dismay.

Just as he thought, mentioning Ellen dumped a bucket of cold water on the evening. Very straight and respectfully, he says, "I better go now, Nicky. Thanks a lot for your kind offer, and for your hospitality."

Nicky is silent. Jim smiles cordially and leaves her boudoir. As soon as she's sure he has descended the stairway, Nicky picks up the telephone and says to the operator, "1647 please." Hearing Albert Beamish answer, she says, "He just left. Nothing happened. I never even got to first base." When she hears Beamish's angry response, she replies, "Hey, forget it, and you don't need to talk to me like that, Albert, because there won't be another chance. The man's engaged to be married. He's a faithful, honest guy, something you wouldn't know too much about." She listens again. "Alright. I'll meet you there at ten tomorrow morning."

Nicky hangs up the phone and puts her head in her hands. "Damn! Wouldn't you know, he's the authentic, real thing."

Chapter 8

Nicky and Beamish are seated in an otherwise empty bar in the Broadway Theater District. "What'll you have, Nicky?"

She tries to hide her disappointment. "After last night's experience I could use a boilermaker, but just order me a Martini."

After giving their order to the waiter, Beamish studies her beautiful, but troubled, face, and says, "Your charms failed, huh?"

She looks Beamish in the eyes, clearly upset by this question. "I did everything but perform a striptease for him, which, as you know very well, is not my style." Then she shakes her head, completely distressed, because she secretly has fallen for everything about Jim.

Oblivious of her feelings, he makes it obvious that he would never turn her down. "I'm sure you were irresistible, as you always are to me. I think he's been out on the prairie so long he's forgotten what a woman is for."

Realizing his meaning, she is cold. "Forget it, Albert. Just tell me what you got me out of bed for at this ungodly hour."

He takes one more furtive look at her as their drinks are served and says, "Well, I've got a plan."

"Look, Albert, Joe Curtain's will dumps the controlling stock in the railroad right in this bumpkin's lap. So what can we do about it? After all, he is the legal heir, provided he kills or captures that crook Arizona Adams." Annoyed, she takes a long sip of the Martini.

"Maybe not."

"Oh, come on, Albert. Face reality!"

"We'll see. Finish your drink and come with me. We're going to see a couple of private investigators I've used in the past for special jobs." Nicky, looking very puzzled, takes a last sip of her drink, accepts Beamish's hand to help her out of her chair, and they leave the bar.

*

About an hour later they're walking down a corridor of the recently opened Flatiron Building, and stop before an office door with the words "Dunigan and Bassett, Very Private Investigating" engraved in gold letters. A receptionist ushers them into the office of Dunigan, a ferret-eyed, middle-aged, corpulent man, who comes from behind his desk with his hand extended to Beamish. "Glad to see you again, Mr. Beamish. Always a great pleasure to do business with you and the Curtain Rail Lines. And this, I take it, is the former Mrs. Curtain, am I right?" He holds out his hand.

She barely touches it. "Nicky Corwin, now. My maiden name."

They take seats in front of the desk, as Dunigan returns to his leather chair and faces them. Smelling money, he is overly ingratiating. "How may we be of help?"

Beamish says, "I told you on the phone about this heir apparent, Jim Courtney."

"Right."

Beamish looks at Nicky and decides to be inclusive. "Nicky and I have reason to believe this fellow may be a con man."

Dunigan gets it. "A con man. I see."

"We need a firm we can trust to carry out a discreet background check on him. You understand, Mr. Dunigan?"

Dunigan gets up, goes to the door to the adjoining office, and calls through the open door, "Mr. Bassett, would you please join us?" A man in his mid-forties, very squat, looking a bit like a boxer dog, enters the room. He was obviously listening to their conversation.

"Yes, Mr. Dunigan?"

Dunigan indicates their clients with a wave of his hand. "Mr. Bassett, this is Nicky Corwin, and you know Mr. Beamish. Folks, this is 'Hound Dog' Bassett. He has more than earned the nickname 'Hound Dog' because when he sinks his teeth into anything, he never lets go. Depend on it."

Hound Dog smiles with something that looks like a baring of teeth. Beamish and Nicky nod back.

With confidence, Dunigan says, "I'll fill you in on the details, later, Hound Dog. Suffice it to say these good people want you to, ah, gather, ah, a bit of information on a certain individual."

Hound Dog says proudly, "My speciality."

Beamish wants to be sure that he understands what is required. "The job will call for travelling to Arizona for a bit, Mr. Hound Dog."

"Please call me Bassett."

Beamish stands corrected. "Of course, Mr. Bassett. The individual in question resides in Whistle Stop, Arizona."

"Whistle Stop? Is that for real?"

"It's for real, all right. All you have to do is check to see if he's ever been in trouble with the law and generally has a good character. Simple enough, eh?" Beamish looks at Bassett man-to-man.

Dunigan jumps in. "Very well. You understand this will involve a retainer and daily expenses?"

Beamish is all business. "Get what we want and there will also be a handsome bonus in it for your firm. Incidentally, and very important, Mr. Hound Dog, you must never indicate in any way, and that includes visiting my hotel room, that you know me while we're in Whistle Stop. Also, use the telegraph to contact Nicky, here. Use a code for her. Call her 'Nicky Shade'. Get it, Nicky Curtain—Nicky Shade." He laughs in appreciation of his own wit.

Dunigan doesn't want to get off course. "The, uh, retainer will be five hundred dollars. Total cost will depend on how much time and effort will be needed. Daily expense, fifty dollars a day. Agreed?"

Beamish looks at Nicky, who nods agreement. Beamish says, "Agreed." Then he writes out a check and hands it to Dunigan.

Dunigan happily looks at the check. "I'll have my secretary type up our agreement and a receipt, which our messenger will deliver to you tomorrow."

Bassett asks, "When do I leave?"

"Thursday morning at 9 A.M. your messenger can pick up your train tickets. And now, gentlemen, we'll be leaving." Beamish shakes hands with Dunigan and Bassett. Nicky smiles and they leave.

As soon as the door closes behind them, Dunigan does a few jubilant dance steps, claps his hands, and slaps Hound Dog on the back. "I love you! An expense account. We're gonna get so fat and be-yoo-ti-ful by landing this job. Take your time in Whistle Stop. We gotta play it for all the law will allow! These two chumps are swimming in moolah!"

Bassett pretends to growl, "Hound Dog is on the trail!"

"Get yourself a ten-gallon hat and bone up on the lingo. Sick 'em, Hound Dog!"

Chapter 9

On the front page of the *New York Tribune,* there is a bold headline over a two-column photo: RAIL LINE EXECS TRACK OUTLAWS. In the photo, the Curtain Rail Lines Directors, wearing ten-gallon hats, with some wearing bandanas, are facing the camera in intrepid poses.

Jim watches from the ferry dock as Beamish and the Directors march into the cavernous hall of the Curtain Lines' New York ferry terminal, followed by a booming military band playing "You're a Grand Old Flag." A crowd of Curtain Rail Lines employees carry banners and signs saying "CURTAINS TO ARIZONA ADAMS" . . . "BULLETS FOR BANDITS" . . . "GOOD HUNTING BOSSMEN!" . . . "WATCH YOUR TAIL—THE RAILMEN ARE ON YOUR TRAIL."

News photographers are snapping pictures, as many Curtain Rail Lines employees follow Beamish, Jim, and the Directors onto the ferry waiting to take them to Jersey City. As they cast off, Jim looks back at the New York City skyline, contemplating the treacherous adventure that lies ahead.

On the Jersey side, the Curtain Rail Lines conductor, Henry Parnell, is amazed at the entourage as he tips his hat to Jim, realizing that maybe he is Mr. Curtain's heir. He looks at a large, dollar pocket-watch, then yells, "All abo-o-oard!" Jim and the Directors board the train, leaving the photographers, crowd, and general hoopla behind.

The train starts with a lurch, then begins to slowly roll out of the station, as Beamish and the Directors wave their ten-gallon hats from the windows of the passenger car they have reserved for themselves. Holding on to his ten-gallon hat, Hound Dog Bassett unobtrusively scrambles to board the very last car of the train.

The train is now rapidly moving through New Jersey, with its whistle blowing as it passes through town after town. Inside their plushly appointed first-class car, a number of the Directors, still in their Western headgear, are gathered around Beamish, who reads aloud the *Wall Street Graphic* story about their mission. Jim is stretched out pretending to be asleep in his seat, with his hat tipped over his face. He's actually listening carefully to the self-involved Directors' comments about the story, and puzzling out various plans for dealing with them—and with Ellen and his Adams Gang once they arrive in Whistle Stop.

Beamish stands up and, seeing that Jim is asleep, he calls out loudly, "We have a long way to go, men, so let's not waste time. I suggest that we use the journey to prepare for meeting the people of Whistle Stop. Will Toomey here used to live out West for a while. He'll conduct the meeting. Please give him your attention. Will . . ."

Will stands up. He is in his mid-fifties, well dressed, with greying hair, and he seems friendly. "Hey, men, I used to live out in Montana with the prairie dogs when I was a young man. Made my first stake there. Trust me, so's you won't stand out like beacon lights in a storm, I'm gonna try to familiarize you with some of the more customary patterns of Western speech. I need somebody to give me a hand. How about you, Henry? You like to do a lot of jawin'."

Henry Travis rises to join Will. He is in his mid-forties and makes up for his small stature by walking with practiced arrogance. Decked out in his ten-gallon hat, he brings a smile to Will's face as he shakes his hand. "Now let's suppose you and I are having a conversation in Whistle Stop, Henry." Will turns to the other Directors and says, "Everybody pay attention and learn—I mean 'larn' something." Keeping his desire to laugh in check when he glances back at Henry, who looks like an overgrown mushroom in his hat, he says, "Howdy, pardner, them is mighty fine duds you're duked out in, ah reckon."

The Directors comment to one another. Some take out expensive pens and notebooks and write the words down.

Will waits until all of their pens are poised. "'Duds' mean clothes. 'Duked out in' means dressed in. And always end up by saying 'Ah reckon'. Maybe you'll remember better if you repeat the words after Henry and me." He spots Jim, who it seems is still asleep. "That thar's Jim Courtney over thar. Him's grabbin' hisself some shut eye."

The Directors, in chorus, say, "Over thar, Jim's grabbin' hisself some shut eye."

Will says to Henry, "Ah see whar the lawmen caught up with them rustlin' varmints."

Henry is into it. "Yup. Surely did. Done give the varmints a necktie party."

The Directors, taking the lesson seriously, repeat each phrase. "Ah see whar the lawmen gave them varmints a necktie party."

Will says, "Good! You hombres are catchin' on real quick."

The Directors say, in unison, "Hombres."

Will gives Henry a big smile and says, "When we git to Whistle Stop, we'll be hankerin' to wet our whistles and grab some grub, ah do believe."

The Directors repeat with gusto, "Hankerin' to wet our whistles and grab some grub."

Will stresses, "Don't forget to add, 'Ah do believe.'"

His pupils respond, "Ah do believe."

Will says, "Henry, ain't you got no choreees to do?"

The Directors repeat, "Choreees."

Very pleased with his fellow Directors, Will is now more conversational. "Well now, boys, ah do reckon ah'll ride out on mah spread an' see if them rustlin' varmints done stole any of mah cayows, unless any uh y'all didn't git the gist of my words."

Felix Herkimer's hand pops up. He says, "A 'spread' . . . that means a ranch or a farm, doesn't it?"

Will nods. "Right, Felix. But don't say 'doesn't', say 'don't it'."

Henry asks, sheepishly, "Just in case it might crop up, how do you say 'girl'?"

The young, chubby director, Dilbert Findley, asks hesitantly, "Young un?"

Henry says, "That can't be right, Dilbert."

"Then how?"

Will settles it. "Always say 'filly', see? And if she's a knockout, she's a 'right purty filly'. Now everybody repeat after me, 'Ain't she a right purty filly'?"

At that moment the door at the front of the car opens, and a middle-aged, very stout matron enters, as the Directors are calling in chorus, "Ain't she a right purty filly?"

The matron, astounded, says, "Why, you fresh old fools!" Then she hastily exits and enters the next car. She stops, takes her mirror from her purse, and looks in it furtively, with suppressed happiness. She fluffs her hair then walks down the aisle of the car, swinging her heavy hips a bit seductively. All the while she's being observed by Hound Dog Bassett, who has been careful to keep a low profile.

Back in the Directors car Beamish takes charge. "That's enough lingo larnin' for now, pardners. There's one more thing, however. In this jerkwater town we're heading for, all the hayseeds ride horses as soon as they quit crawling on the floor. So they all walk bowlegged. That being so, we all better practice the Western walk, so we won't stand out too much. Let me show you what I mean."

Beamish gets out of his seat and walks up and down the aisle, with a grotesque rendition of what he thinks is the Western walk. When he finishes, all the Directors get in line and start practicing the Western walk and talk. Jim, who has been listening to this ridiculous charade while pretending to be asleep, peeks out from under the brim of his hat. He can hardly hold back from splitting his sides laughing, as he watches the Curtain Rail Lines Directors make fools of themselves.

Chapter 10

Jim would not be smiling at all if he were able to witness what was taking place at that very moment between Grady Profit and Sage near his Arizona Adams' hideout. They are standing at the edge of a precipice having a serious argument. Grady is fuming. "When the hell is he comin' back, Sage?"

Sage, defending Arizona, says in a strong voice, "Jeez Grady, what Arizona do and don't do ain't none of yer bees wax. 'Sides, it's only been a little over a week. Sometimes he stays away for two, mebbe three weeks."

"While we go nuts twiddlin' our thumbs."

"Watch it, Grady, Arizona's got his reasons."

He answers right back, tough and mean, "And I got mine. If he ain't back here in a week, I'm takin' over the gang."

Sage tries to reason with him. "Look, Grady, you know the men are dangerous. Arizona's the boss and the only one can control 'em."

"Won't need no control when I take over. And we ain't gonna just take no measly fines from them fool passengers. We'll take everything of value off of them. Any passenger gits outta line gits a bullet! And we'll blow the safe on the train, too. I got some dynamite cached away. "

"Arizona put me in charge, so none of that's happenin'. Not while I'm around, Grady! We're done here." Sage turns to walk back to the hideout.

Grady watches Sage's back for only a second and then growls, "That's right! Not while yer around." Then like a wild cat, Grady takes a few fast steps toward Sage and pushes him violently forward. Sage pitches out over the edge of the cliff and hurtles to the rocks far below. Grady looks down at the inert body, and then heads back to the hideout cabin.

*

At just about the same time, Ellen is seated at Jim's desk in the *Gazette* office working on a story. A telegraph messenger boy arrives.

"Telegram for you, Miss Ellen."

Taking it from the boy, she says, "Thanks, Tom," and reads the telegram as he leaves. Then she walks over to the pressroom door and calls out to Charley, "Hey, got a telegram from Jim. He says the Directors of the Curtain Rail Lines are scheduled to arrive here with him on Monday's 4 P.M. train. We have to get out a special edition."

Charlie doesn't bother looking up from his work. "Right."

As Ellen sits at the desk to write the story on her Remington typewriter, she's plenty curious about this development.

*

Later in the afternoon, a crowd of townspeople are gathered in the town square around a shopkeeper who's reading aloud from the *Gazette.* "'The Curtain Lines board of directors is to arrive here on the Monday afternoon train. Let's give them a Whistle Stop welcome. They will reveal the details of their mission when they arrive.' What in Hallelujah you figger them Eastern dudes is comin' for?"

Another man says, "Beats me."

A nicely dressed rancher pipes in, "Smells fishy! These varmints is up to sumpin' big, you can bet on that!"

As the crowd disperses, one man mutters suspiciously to his wife, "Whatta those fat cats gonna do, charge us for havin' their railroad pass through town? They already robbed plenty off the old time ranchers for that."

She hits him in the arm. "What is the matter with you, Horace, cain't you see they're after that train robber, Arizona Adams? I'm glad they're comin' to rid us of that menace. My cousin Violet in Chicago is too scared to come visit us 'cause of him."

Chapter 11

The following Monday the Curtain Rail Lines train is approaching Whistle Stop. The conductor enters the Directors car, calling out, "Whistle Stop, next."

The Directors and Jim, who are all sprawled out on their seats or sleeping, suddenly sit upright as the train slowly pulls into the depot. The Directors, still dressed in their fancy New York suits, look out the windows at the crowd of townspeople. The women are in simple, early-summer pastel dresses, and the men are dressed in Western suits or cowpoke attire. They are carrying signs saying:

"WELCUM TO CURTAIN RAIL BRASS!"
"WHISTLE STOP SAYS HI DIRECTORS!"

The train comes to a grinding, steam-erupting stop.

Beamish steps off first, followed by the other Directors who—rather apprehensively—file out, wearing their ten-gallon hats, doing their Western walk, and carrying their expensive suitcases. They're followed by Jim, who immediately searches for Ellen but doesn't see her in the crowd.

Mayor Kibbee, in his late forties, dressed in his finest duds, and Sheriff Lynch, with his scruffy, greying hair peeking out of his well-worn, ten-gallon hat, and his gun belt hanging low under his bulging belly, stand expectantly before the lustily cheering crowd.

A few over-excited cowboys blast their six-shooters in the air, to the horror of the Directors, who immediately duck in unison, fearful of being shot by this wild crowd. Mayor Kibbee, unfazed by the crowd's antics, steps up with his hand extended to Beamish. "Welcum, welcum to Whistle Stop. I'm Mayor Kibbee, and this here is Sheriff Lynch. We're right happy to have you all visit our town."

Cordially shaking hands with each of them, Beamish says, "We thank you, kindly. I'm Albert Beamish, current chairman of the board of the Curtain Rail Lines. Mighty pleased to meet you both."

Mayor Kibbee and Sheriff Lynch steer the Directors over to the town square, where they have hastily set up a four-foot-high platform, normally used for cattle auctions. Jim follows them up the makeshift stairs, puzzled that Ellen is not there to greet him.

People in the crowd yell, "Speech! Speech! Speech!" Still amazed by the size of the crowd, Beamish reluctantly takes center stage.

Jim's face lights up when he finally spots Ellen frantically waving to him, as she makes her way through the crowd to the platform. Jim helps her up the stairs and, in full view of all those assembled, they embrace and give each other a long kiss hello. Jim says, "Hi darlin', did you miss me?" She laughs, and they kiss again.

Mayor Kibbee fans his face with his bowler hat as he watches Jim and Ellen kiss, then, putting his hat back on, he raises his arms to get the attention of the exuberant crowd. "All right, folks, let's settle down and show these here Directors of the Curtain Rail Lines the gracious hospitality our town is so famous for." Pointing to Beamish, he continues, "This gentleman here, Mr. Albert Beamish, will address you and give us all the inside story of why they are favorin' us with their presence. Let's give them a big Whistle Stop welcum!"

With that the crowd goes wild again.

"Yeah!"

"Wahoooooo!"

"Yipee!"

"Speech! Speech! Speech!"

Kibbee says to Beamish, "Go on, sir."

Not prepared with a speech, Beamish, looking decidedly pale around the gills, inches cautiously forward, clears his throat, and begins speaking. "Ladies and gentlemen of the beautiful town of Whistle Stop . . ."

The crowd cheers again at the mention of Whistle Stop.

Beamish takes out his handkerchief and wipes his brow, as the commotion dies down. Now smiling at the appreciation, he continues, "We want to thank you for your heartfelt welcome and tell you how happy we are to be here in the golden West! Nothing can compare . . ."

Virgil, a bearded, old prospector holding a half-empty bottle of whiskey, turns to an equally drunken citizen, exclaiming in a loud voice, "Gold 'n the West! See what I tole ya, Clem, these Eastern dudes wouldn' be here 'cept for the fact they musta struck gold up in the hills. Mebbe the old gold mine out near Reedville."

Oblivious, Beamish continues. ". . . to the hearts of gold to be found everywhere in the golden West!"

While Virgil's drunk buddy Clem nods and says in an equally loud voice, "Yer right, Virgil! They found gold!"

Word quickly spreads in the crowd.

"They struck gold!"

"It's a big gold strike!"

"That's why these crooks are here."

Virgil yells out, "There ain't nothin' to compare with the gold they found!" This sets off another round of comments.

"I want some of that gold!"

"Whar's that gold?"

"These dudes cain't jes show up and take our gold!"

Beamish, now aware that the crowd has turned, struggles to continue speaking, as their uproar grows. "My comrades-in-arms here . . . are all members of the board of directors of the Curtain Rail Lines. Even though we are not gunfighters, we are convinced we are more than a match for Arizona Adams and his gang, because of our superiority in strategic manoeuvring. I promise you that in the end we shall triumph. That is our purpose for being here. This Adams Gang has been terrorizing you golden-hearted folks long enough. Now that we're here, their days of robbing honest folks are drawing to a close!"

With that, a town mischief maker, Tommy, about ten years old, takes out his slingshot, aims at Beamish, lets loose with a pellet, and then quickly hides his slingshot.

Beamish, hit on the neck, whirls around.

A pig squeals loudly, and a mangy dog howls, while the town folks get more and more riled up.

Virgil talks over everyone. "Who theys kiddin' with that capturing Arizona Adams manure? They ain't no match for a bunch of old ladies with broomsticks! They're here fer the gold!"

Finishing a nip from his bottle, Clem shouts, "Whar's the gold? They ain't said whar the gold strike is! Whar's the gold strike?"

Virgil shouts, "They ain't about to tell us! They wanna keep all the gold for theyselves, after I've been breakin' my back for twenty years!"

Beamish continues, thinking that the word gold has struck a chord with the crowd. "Gold? The gold, my friends, is in your hearts!"

Tommy lets loose and pelts Beamish again. He grabs his neck, as the momentum of the crowd's anger grows. "Whar's the gold? Whar's the gold? Ya claim-jumpers better cut us in!"

Clem, now very drunk, slurs out, "They ain't sayin' whar the claim is. Wanna keep it all for theyselves!"

Virgil, now on the warpath, yells, "Right you are, Clem! Let's string 'em up, hang 'em high! Damn dudes! Stealin' our gold. Come on, boys!"

Suddenly, lassos begin flying through the air. One drops around Beamish's neck. The mob storms the platform, grabs the Directors, and runs them off toward a grove of scruffy trees at the edge of the town square, where several angry men begin to throw ropes over heavy tree limbs.

Jim says frantically to Sheriff Lynch, "Put a stop to this! They're making a mistake! There's no gold strike!"

Sheriff Lynch responds, "Are ya sure? They seem guilty to me."

Jim grabs Beamish's suitcase and breaks it open. The *Wall Street Graphic* newspaper, featuring the picture of the Curtain Rail Lines Directors' and story about their mission to face the Adams Gang, is right on top of his clothes. Jim pulls it out and shows it to the Sheriff and Mayor Kibbee. "Quick, show them this!"

The two Whistle Stop officials look at the paper but make no move to stop the lynchers. The Directors—now with nooses around their necks—are terrified beyond belief. Jim quickly pulls the Sheriff's gun from his holster and fires four shots over the heads of the crowd. The would-be lynchers freeze and stare at Jim. Still pointing the gun in the air, Jim yells at Sheriff Lynch, "Sheriff, show 'em now or I'm gonna have to stop this any way I can!"

For a split second, the Sheriff looks like he's hankerin' for a necktie party, but then sees the wisdom of Jim's righteousness, and yells over to Virgil and his crowd of vigilantes, "Cut it out, boys!" He holds the paper up high. "See, they ain't found gold. This is what they come here for. Like that dude Beamish said, they're out to git Arizona Adams! Thas all."

As the crowd gathers around, looking at the newspaper, various voices are heard from men who can actually read.

"I'll be . . . no gold?"

"Them sissies is out to git Arizona?"

"They'll be goners fer sure!"

"Aw shucks, no necktie party."

Virgil, who can't read, is still suspicious of the Directors. "Thas jes a cover up. I'll be a watchin' ya. "

The truth of the matter dawns on the rest of them. Reluctantly, they disperse, shaking their heads in disbelief. Some laugh and talk among themselves at the idea that these Eastern fuddy-duddies think they can go up against Arizona Adams and his gang.

Jim hands the sheriff his gun and gives him a strong look. Lynch puts it in his holster and walks over to take the rope from around Beamish's neck. "Sorry, Mr. Director. I'm fixin' on talkin' to them varmints that done started this whole lynchin' business." With that, he saunters off in the direction of the saloon.

As Beamish rubs his neck, Mayor Kibbee says to him, "I apologize for our citizenry. I expect you'll be wantin' to relax in nice surroundings? Rooms has been reserved fer you all at the Assay Hotel down Main Street." Jim and the mayor help the other Directors with taking the ropes from around their necks. Scared and none too happy about their so-called Whistle Stop welcome, or even coming to Whistle Stop to begin with, they pick up their suitcases and follow Mayor Kibbee, Jim, and Ellen down Main Street to the hotel.

The Assay Hotel, built about fifty years ago for the gold rush, is the largest building on Main Street. It's a big, wide, ramshackle affair, displaying a weather-beaten old wooden sign. The last two letters of the hotel name have come loose over time and slipped down, so that what the eye sees is: ASS HOTEL AND SALOON. Obviously not a high-class establishment, there are two entrances, one to the hotel and one to the saloon.

Jim says to the travel-weary Directors, "You men get cleaned up. I'm heading over to the *Gazette* office. I'll see you later."

The Directors have pulled themselves together enough to take a good leer at Ellen, who is standing behind Jim. Realizing that he can't escape introducing her to them, he takes Ellen's arm. "I'd like to introduce you to my *fiancée*, Miss Ellen Williams."

All of the Directors take off their hats. Several say in unison, "Right nice to meet you, Miss Williams."

"Nice to meet you too. Believe me, I wish you every success in capturing Arizona Adams."

Jim tips his hat to them and walks away with Ellen.

The Directors put their hats back on and follow Mayor Kibbee into the hotel. Will Toomey says, "Now she's a right purty filly."

Dilbert Finley adds his approval. "Jim Courtney sure knows how to pick 'em."

Beamish stops to take one last look at Jim and Ellen walking down the street, knowing that there is tough work ahead. He then spies Hound Dog Bassett following them discreetly on the other side of the street. Satisfied that the detective is on the case, he enters the hotel.

Chapter 12

The Directors look around and are immediately shocked at the filthy, shabby lobby. There are a few stuffed armchairs, an old sofa, and a table. To the left is a hallway leading to somewhere in the back, and off to the right is a door into the saloon. A grizzled room clerk is snoozing behind an old reception desk.

Mayor Kibbee pokes him. "Got them rooms ready, Luke?"

Luke wakes with a start, taking in the mayor and the well-dressed Eastern Directors. "Rooms, Rooms? Oh! Sure 'nuff, mayor. Whole first floor. Take any rooms you fancy, gents. Ain't nobody but coupla old ladies roomin' jist now, first door on the right. Off season, y'know." Luke hands out keys.

The Directors troop upstairs carrying their expensive suitcases, complaining about the dirt. The mayor calls after them, "You fellas take care. I'll be seeing you soon."

At the top of the stairs, Beamish opens the first room door on the left and a cloud of dust greets him. The other Directors carry on down the hallway and enter various rooms, each room emitting a cloud of dust.

Beamish enters his room and exhibits great distaste. He looks around and sees it is small with a dusty, cracked, and broken window, a torn old shade hanging down, a scarred bureau, a chipped porcelain pitcher on the washbowl, and a rumpled, unmade bed.

Brushing off his suit he mutters, "My God!" He immediately goes out in the hallway to the top of the stairs and looks down at the reception desk. He sees that the mayor is gone now and the old room clerk, Luke, with his chair tipped back against the wall, is cleaning his nails with a penknife. He calls down to the clerk, "Sir! Mister!"

Old Luke comes from behind the counter and looks up at Beamish. "Yessir?"

"I need maid service. As quick as possible!"

Luke is puzzled but polite. "Maid service, you say?" He thinks for a minute as Beamish looks down at him, then wanting to please, he says, "Yessir, right away, sir."

Beamish responds curtly, "Please hurry her right up here." He returns to his room.

Luke leans on the counter with his chin cupped in his hands, looking extremely puzzled, muttering to himself, "Maid service? Maid service?" Then his eyes light up.

A short while later, Beamish is busy using his own handkerchief to wipe out one the drawers from the bureau. There is a knock on the door. Beamish calls out, "One minute, please." He opens the door and sees a brassy blonde wearing a very low-cut spangled dress, hardly concealing overflowing, enticing breasts. She is one of the dance hall prostitutes, but he's not aware of this.

The blonde, in a seductive tone, purrs, "Hello, you sent for me?"

Beamish, slightly surprised, is obviously doubtful about her housekeeping abilities. "Well, yes, please come in." The blonde comes into the room, closes the door, and sits down on the bed. She hikes up her dress, revealing a very shapely pair of legs, which Beamish ogles. Then pulling himself together, he says expectantly, "Well, that's the bed."

The blonde pats the bed. "Feels comfortable."

Beamish is officious as he always is with hired help. "Yes. As you can see, I need your services quickly."

She smiles. "I can see that."

Beamish takes off his tie, sits down on the rickety chair, and removes his shoes.

The blonde says, "How long would you want this to be?"

Beamish looks up at her. "Well, as long as it takes. I'll pay for extra time. I don't want anything dirty, you know."

She's a bit indignant. "I should hope not!"

Glad that she has pride in her work, he ponders for a few seconds, then says, "I would say it can be finished in about two or three hours."

She's astonished. "Two or three hours?!"

He looks around the filthy room. "Well, if you like, you can do half of it now and the other half tomorrow."

Now she's smiling. "A two day job! Then we better get started right away, mister!" She gets up and starts lowering her shoulder straps.

"Wait a minute! What are you gonna do?"

Flashing a big smile at him, she says, "Whatever you say, honey."

Suddenly he comprehends. "Oh, my gosh! I just wanted . . ." Realizing that there's no point in explaining, he takes out his wallet and gives her fifteen dollars. "Thanks a lot, sweetheart, but on second thought I'd just better do it myself."

Now she's shocked. "You'll do it yourself?" She pulls up her shoulder straps, quickly walks to the door, and, as she leaves, says sarcastically, "Enjoy yourself, honey. You don't know what you're missing."

The blonde comes down the stairs. Sporting a big smile, old Luke asks, "How was the old turkey? Not much, I'd say, judgin' by the short time you was with him."

"Dunno, Luke. He wanted to do it by himself. Maybe that's why he looks the way he does! But he gave me fifteen bucks for nothin'." She reaches in her purse and drops a few bits on the counter for Luke. "Thanks!" They have a good laugh before she saunters back toward the saloon door, passing none other than Hound Dog Bassett, who gives her a hard look, as he enters the hotel and walks up to Luke to register.

Chapter 13

Jim and Ellen are on horseback, riding along a beautiful trail near town. "It's good to have you back again, Jim. Even if you really don't own the railroad—which, as far as I'm concerned, will never happen now, given the proviso in your uncle's will."

Hearing her determination, and still having no plans to clue her in on his real dilemma, Jim tries to reassure her. "Well, darlin', don't be thinkin' about that, because I haven't decided yet about how I'm gonna deal with the proviso."

Her eyes widen with fear as she quickly and emphatically says, "Well I have some news that will help you decide right quick. While you were gone, the Arizona Adams Gang hit the Curtain Lines again. But this time it was a lot different than ever before."

He gives her his full attention. "How so?"

"They not only robbed all the passengers of their jewels and money, but they shot two of them who resisted, and blew the safe, to boot."

He's shocked and surprised. "What?"

Glad that she has now gained his keen interest, she says, "You heard me, Jim, and they got away with the money and valuables in the safe, and those two passengers almost died."

Angrily, under his breath, he curses Grady. "Damn, him!"

Thinking he means Arizona, and already worried that Jim might consider fulfilling the terms of Joe Curtain's will, she presses the advantage this news has given her. "So now will you please forget about Arizona Adams and your uncle's proviso?"

Stone faced—not wanting to reveal the extent of his anger at Grady and the gang—he says, "Maybe."

"No 'maybe', Jim. Arizona's not worth getting yourself killed over, and that's that. So let's both relax and drop this topic. Why don't you come out to the ranch for dinner tonight? Mom and dad would like that, and you can tell us all about your adventures in the Big City."

Looking at her beautiful face melts away his troubles for the moment. "I'd like that a lot."

*

As the setting sun paints the Western sky with colors of red, orange, and purple, Jim rides the few miles out to the Williams' ranch, deep in thought about what has happened to his old friend Sage in his absence. He knows that Sage never would have allowed Grady and the gang to shoot passengers, or take more than the twenty-five dollar fines. And how should he proceed with the Directors? As he rides past the Williams' grazing cattle towards their cozy ranch house, he concludes that, for now, he'll need to deal with the details on a day-by-day basis. He dismounts and hitches his horse in front of the neatly kept flower beds and the vegetable garden sprouting corn, tomatoes, lettuce, and herbs.

As Jim steps through the front door, he is greeted very affectionately by the lovely Helen Williams and her husband Glen, who looks pretty pale to Jim. Ellen kisses him hello. The ranch house living room is neat and warm. Glen Williams is mighty curious. "Well, Jim, we are sure waiting to hear about your adventure in New York City."

"Let's get started with the story at dinner, Jim." Helen Williams takes her future son-in-law's arm and leads him to the dining room.

*

Discreetly skipping the story about Glad at the Cafe Splendide, and only referring to Nicky as his uncle's much younger ex-wife, Jim has had them laughing at the Directors' foolishness since he has met them, and is now retelling their Western-walking-and-talking schoolroom antics on the train, as they are finishing dessert. "You had to be there, but trust me, it took a lot of discipline to not burst out laughing as I watched them walking up and down the train, over and over for hundreds of miles, trying to walk the cowboy walk. They even went over the best method and coached each other. They are such egotistical, annoying men. Especially Beamish." With that, Jim pushes back from the table with a satisfied smile on his face. "On a far more important topic, I've been dreaming of a dinner like that, Helen!"

Helen smiles at the compliment. "Thank you, Jim, but you know darn well with all the dinners you've had here that Ellen's a better cook than I am."

"No, mom, it was you that taught me. I'm merely your star pupil."

Glen, who obviously loves the two ladies in his life, interrupts them with a worried look. "Say, Jim, this Beamish fellow you've been tellin' us about, fact is, his name rings a bell with me. You remember that letter we got from the Curtain Rail Lines, Helen? Wasn't that signed by an Albert Beamish?"

"I remember the letter only too well, Glen. Let me think." Her eyes light up. "You're right! It was Albert Beamish. Oh dear, Glen, I'm afraid he's up to no good, coming out here." Helen and Glen share a serious look.

Jim's deeply concerned. "Good God, if you don't mind my asking, what did it say?"

Glen looks Jim in the eyes for a moment, then gets up to get a humidor filled with cigars from the buffet and offers it to Jim. "Care for a cigar, Jim?" Jim shakes his head no, still waiting on his answer. Glen takes one, strikes a match and is about to light up.

Ellen bolts to his side. "Dad, what are doing?" She takes the cigar from his hand.

Glen reluctantly blows out the match. "I forgot."

Ellen scolds, "You can't afford to forget, dad." Glen looks back to Helen, then glances away, having no intention of telling Jim about their problems.

Ellen, obviously concerned about her dad, asks Jim, "Would you like to take a walk? There's a big, beautiful waxing moon out tonight."

Seeing that she needs to talk with him about what just happened, he obliges. "Well, that's a fine offer. Would you two please excuse us?"

*

As they walk outside, Ellen takes Jim's hand and leads him down the path toward the corral, where they stop to look at the moon. They are both quiet and deep in thought for a while. Then Jim asks, "Is your dad okay, Ellen? He seems a bit off his feed to me."

She looks away, over the stark, moon-illuminated flatlands. "Well . . . he's under strict doctor's orders to take it easy since his heart attack a few weeks ago."

"That's why you snatched that cigar from him?"

She is upset, as she slowly opens up to Jim. "Yes. He's under terrible pressure right now. It's that letter they talked about from that Mr. Beamish."

Jim presses her. "Will you please tell me about the letter? Please!"

She looks up at him. "It's about the mortgage on the ranch. You know that the drought last year killed off a lot of our cattle. I told you we came out with a loss, Jim, but I didn't tell you how big. It's big enough—dad hasn't been able to meet the last two mortgage payments, and we're about to skip the next one. You know that the Curtain Rail Lines holds the mortgages on most of the land around here, including our house and ranch. Well, even though Mr. Watson at the bank wants to help us, that Mr. Beamish has been threatening foreclosure if we don't make up those pay-ments, which we can't possibly do until the fall roundup. So, I know it was worry that brought on dad's heart attack."

Jim stomps around, cursing, "That damned, son-of-a-gun." Then he looks at Ellen's shocked face and takes hold of her hands. "Darlin', why on earth didn't you tell me all this before?"

"Dad made me promise. You know him. He didn't want to burden you with this."

"Now I understand why you seemed so worried about the Curtain Rail Lines the day I got the lawyer's letter about being my uncle's heir." He thinks for a minute, then quickly makes up his mind. "So . . . I have something I need to tell you." She looks up at his determined face with curiosity. "Well, the truth is, Ellen, I heard what you said about the proviso this afternoon. And I'm not gonna pretend that I wouldn't be badly disappointed about not taking over the rail line. I could probably forget about it in time. But I'll never forget that my parents and a whole bunch of folks already lost their ranches to the Curtain Lines—ironically at the hands of my dead uncle—nor that your dad survived the first wave of their greed, and built this ranch up from wild scrubland over a long period of hard working years and plenty of danger. So, if he lost it now, when he should be enjoying his rewards, well . . . I think he might . . ."

She cuts in. "Have another heart attack?"

With deep concern, he replies, "I hate to say it, Ellen. But yes—maybe his last."

Tears start to well in her eyes. "Oh, Jim!" She leans her head on his chest, sobbing softly.

He strokes her hair. "Don't you worry, darlin', it's not gonna happen."

Looking up, suddenly apprehensive, she says, "Wait just a minute, you're not telling me you're thinking of going up against Arizona?"

Speaking philosophically, he says, "If the Curtain Rail Lines became mine . . ."

She's dead set against this idea. "Oh, please, Jim! It's too high a price to pay!"

"If you lose your father—*and* the ranch . . ."

She voices her strong protest. "I won't hear of it, Jim! You're no match for Arizona Adams. He's a professional gunslinger. You can't call him out, and you're no back shooter. If you ride out after him, he and his gang could ambush you. You'd have no chance!" She sobs. "I couldn't bear it if I lost you."

He smiles down at her with confidence, while he gently wipes away her tears. "Tell your dad to tear up the letter from that skunk Beamish. And don't you worry, darlin', I'm a lot better with a gun than I used to be. I've been making a hobby of target shooting for quite a while now. That's one of the things I've been doing on those private rides of mine."

Seeing there is no sense in arguing with him, she says, "When you set your jaw that way and get that look in your eyes, I know you're going to go ahead no matter what. Oh, Jim . . . you must stop to think . . ." He kisses her and puts an end to the discussion. She melts in his arms.

Chapter 14

At the Whistle Stop jail house early the next morning, Sheriff Lynch is sitting at his beat-up desk playing solitaire when Hound Dog Bassett comes walking through the door. Looking up, the sheriff says, "Mornin', pardner. What may I do fer ya?"

Hound Dog Bassett takes off his hat. "Mornin', sheriff. I want to report a robbery."

The sheriff looks down and moves a column of cards, as he says, "And who may you be?"

"My name is Charles Bassett. I'm staying at the Assay Hotel. Just arrived last night. I'm from Chicago. Unfortunately, I ran into this nasty little problem, which I am sure is a rare occurrence in your fine town, sir."

The sheriff now pays attention and leans back in his chair. "Well, I dunno if I kin help ya, Mr. Basket. Give me the details."

Bassett shifts from one leg to the other pretending embarrassment as he starts spinning his tale. "Have to admit I foolishly left the door to my room unlocked while I went down to the saloon and had a little tequila. Wasn't gone any more'n about a half hour. Well, sheriff, I had left my Ingersoll watch on the chest-of-drawers. When I come back it was gone. Looked everywhere I could think of, but couldn't find it. It's been stolen, all right. "

Sheriff Lynch writes on a pad, "Ingersoll watch." Then he asks, "Long 'bout what time?"

Bassett scratches his head. "I'd say 'bout 9 to 9:30 P.M."

"'Proximate value?"

"Oh, priceless, sheriff. Family heirloom, y'know."

"Okay, Mr. Basket, I'll keep my eyes peeled fer it."

"Thank you, sheriff. I sure 'preciate it."

Bassett starts to leave and, apparently as an after-thought, snaps his fingers and says, "Sheriff, I'm in Whistle Stop as a purchasing agent for a very large meat processing company in Chicago. I've heard some of the best stock comes from areas around here. Any you could recommend?"

The sheriff ponders. "Lemme see. Best we have to offer in these parts is Glen Williams' livestock. Yessir, Glen has some mighty fine cattle on his spread. His daughter, Ellen, is associate editor at the *Whistle Stop Gazette*. You might drop in to talk to her about it."

"I've read that paper at the hotel," Bassett replies. "In fact, I've been thinking about placing an ad in the paper. Isn't the editor a fellow name of Jim Courtney?"

"Yup."

Bassett acts like he's searching his memory. "Jim Courtney, Jim Courtney, seems to me I heard some nice things about him."

"Nicest feller you'd ever want to meet. We'd all like to see him run for mayor of Whistle Stop."

Hound Dog, taking his job seriously, says, "Yes. If everybody was as honest as I hear he is, we'd have a wonderful world."

"Yup."

Bassett presses. "Bet you never had any trouble with him."

"Trouble with Jim? He never done nothin', not one single little thing ever caused trouble for nobody. Honest as they come."

"Well now, that is a miracle! Usually, even in the best of men, there's some little dark secret. But not Jim Courtney! Not one little thing you can think of? Never was part of nothing involving the law?"

Now Sheriff Lynch is scratching his head while he's thinking. "Nope." Then suddenly he remembers an incident. "Well, there wuz *one* little thing, now I recollect . . ."

Hound Dog is very interested. "Really? What was the charge?"

"Rustlin'."

Bassett's astounded. "Rustling?"

"Yup. I disremembered 'cause it was quite some time back."

Hound Dog Bassett is now quite concerned. "Rustling is a very serious charge!"

"Yup. But we caught him, me and a posse."

"I see, I see. And what was the outcome?"

"We strung him up, hanged him higher than an eagle's nest."

Bassett is suddenly very confused. "Hanged him?"

The sheriff is satisfied with what happened. "Yup. Boys got plumb out of hand and strung him up. The varmint is pushin' up daisies in an unmarked grave at the town limits."

"But he's still . . ."

"He's still, all right. Couldn't be stiller. Jim was involved in that incident with the law. He tried to stop the boys from stringin' the varmint up without a trial, but the boys was loaded and out for blood. Jim really tried, though. Even threatened to shoot the guys 'less they backed off. But there was just too many wild ones in the bunch. Anyways, that was 'bout the only time Jim was involved with the law."

Hound Dog Bassett is completely disappointed. "Oh."

The sheriff looks at his notes. "Well, now, Mr. Basket. I'll git right on your case of the stole watch."

Masking his utter frustration, Bassett says, "Yeah, thanks a million. I just can't tell you what a help you've been." He slams his ten-gallon hat on his head and leaves. Under his breath he mutters, "Thanks for nothing!"

Chapter 15

Later that same afternoon, at a makeshift shooting range near town, Jim is in the process of teaching the Directors how to shoot their pistols. Bottles are lined up on a stone wall for target practice. As the Directors take their positions, Mayor Kibbee and Sheriff Lynch ride up to join them. The mayor yells out, "Afternoon! You fellers has all been issued guns now. But since you are going after Arizona and his gang, everythin' must be done by the letter of the law. So Sheriff Lynch will now deputize you. You too, Jim."

Sheriff Lynch gets off of his horse slowly, walks over to them with some ceremony, and says, rather pompously, "Like Mayor Kibbee says, everythin' must be done legal. Raise yer right hand." They all comply. "Now by my aw-thor-ity I do aw-thor-ize, lee-gal-ize, and dep-i-tize you brave men to seek out and destroy Arizona Adams and his gang, and to abide by the laws of the Arizona Territory. There, yer all legal now."

Jim lowers his hand, holding back a wry smile. Sheriff Lynch nods to the mayor, who is pleased and says with authority, "You are now under the protection of the majesty of the law."

Now the Sheriff addresses the Directors man-to-man, with extreme practicality. "Ah have arranged with our local funeral parlor, in case it should be approp-ri-ate, to have yer remains shipped at low cost to yer hometown; or you kin be planted, ah mean buried, here in Whistle Stop, whatever the rail line directs, if it is necessitated. Y'all will be given a deeg-nee-fied eulogy so's ya won't be ashamed afterwards. Only the good stuff ya done will be mentioned, none of the rotten stuff. Also, yer next of kin will be notified."

Henry Travis, a very small, wizened fellow, smiles in a sickly manner at Dilbert Finley, who is beside him and promptly faints, falling to the ground. For a moment the other Directors stare at the sheriff with numb dread, then they revive Henry and give him some water from a canteen Jim provides.

The mayor is relieved that he's okay. Sheriff Lynch salutes smartly. "Well, men, sorry 'bout that, but thems the facts of life 'round these parts. Good luck."

Mayor Kibbee says, "We're much obliged to you. Carry on." With that he and the sheriff mount up and head for town.

After a minute of silence, Jim yells out, "There's only one way to make sure you never need those services, men, and that's practice!" They quickly turn and face the bottles in a single line, holding their pistols out before them. Jim waits to see that they are all ready, then says, "At my signal, fire." He pauses. "Fire!" They all shoot, and when the smoke clears, not one bottle has been hit, but one is swaying and finally topples over. Then a small bird falls out of a nearby tree.

Jim sees a burly, drunken onlooker is laughing his head off. It is the same old geezer prospector, Virgil, who started the gold rush rumor. It's now apparent he followed them out of town just to make sure they weren't doing any prospecting for gold. Jim shakes his head and sighs. "First thing you boys have to learn is not to shut your eyes when you pull the trigger. And squeeze the trigger, don't jerk it. So try once again." A couple of them blink their eyes. Jim yells, "Ready?" They line themselves up again. "Fire!"

As the Directors shoot, Virgil, standing behind them, also fires, and when the smoke clears, the Directors are elated that every bottle has been shattered. They don't realize the burly marksman was responsible for the broken bottles. Now he's standing behind them looking innocent, while the Directors are congratulating one another.

Jim is amazed. "I don't believe it!" He puts new bottle targets on the wall, while the Directors take their stance, all pointing their loaded guns. Jim turns around and sees all their guns pointed at him.

"Boys, be plum sure to wait for the signal." Jim scurries back behind them. "Fire!"

The Directors fire, and when the smoke clears, all the bottles are still standing. Virgil is laughing his head off. Jim, now seeing what is happening, aims his gun at Virgil and motions for him to move away. "Why don't you mount up and get out of here." None too pleased, Virgil gets on his mule and hightails it to town, as Jim focuses on the Directors. "Well, men, you still have a ways to go. Let's try again, because tomorrow morning we'll get started on Arizona's trail."

At the mention of Arizona, the Directors get off a barrage of rounds for the next half hour, but show little improvement. Jim shakes his head in disbelief. "Well, men, that's enough fireworks for now. I suggest that we all steady our nerves at the Assay bar."

Relieved, they all climb into a large open wagon Jim hired from the horse barn, and head back to town for the hotel saloon.

Hound Dog Bassett, who has been watching the whole time from behind some rocks, waits discreetly before mounting his hired horse, and follows them back to town.

Chapter 16

Jim sheepishly follows the Directors, who are walking their version of the Western walk into the Assay Saloon. Cowpokes in the crowded barroom nudge each other to take a gander at the Directors waddling across the room and lining up at the bar. As widespread laughter breaks out, Jim goes to the rear of the room to talk to one of the bar girls he knows.

Unaware that the joke is on them, Beamish raises his glass. "Here's to fine marksmanship, boys." They all down their drinks. Director Felix Herkimer notices a poker game going on in a corner of the barroom. He walks his Western walk over to them and stands watching the players, a very rough-looking bunch.

A stubble-faced card player, after a minute or two, addresses him. "You like to set in, pardner?"

Felix is nervous, "Uh, no thanks. I'll just watch."

The guy looks up, unsmiling. "Kinda makes me a little jumpy, anybody lookin' over mah shoulder."

Another player, in a plaid shirt and vest, pipes in, "Me, too. Either git in or git out!"

Felix, now even more nervous, says deferentially, "Sorry, gents. No harm intended. I'll just be getting along now. You boys enjoy . . ."

A third card player, who has been looking Felix over and figures him for a patsy, jumps in. "I don't believe the dude likes us. Wassa matter, buster, we ain't yer type? Here we are, offerin' you our hospitality and you wanna split." He gives a mean look.

Felix is frightened now. "I never meant . . ."

The heavy-set, fourth player jumps in. "Then set yerself down and jine us in a friendly hand or two." He smirks, pulls back an empty chair, and Felix, thoroughly intimidated, sits down.

The stubble-faced player makes the introductions. "Ahm Cisco." He goes around the table, starting with the dude in the plaid shirt. "This here is Pecos, Mad Dog, and Big Bill. What's yer handle, stranger?"

Nervously genial, he looks around at the four cowboys, then responds, "Felix Herkimer."

With that, Mad Dog starts up. "Did I hear you say 'Felix'? Knew a mama's boy one time had a pussycat named Felix."

Cisco takes his gun out of his holster but then puts it back. "Nah, I wouldn't feel right killin' a dude named Felix. It'd kinda be like shootin' an unarmed woman."

Felix, suddenly remembering the language lessons on the train, says cordially, "Ah reckon as how ahm mighty glad to meet up with you old horned toads, ah do believe."

Now Mad Dog reaches for his gun. "Wassat? You callin' us toads?"

Pecos grabs Mad Dog's hand. "Easy, Mad Dog. You kin see he don't rightly know what he's sayin'."

Felix is confused. "No, no, not toads—cayows!"

Big Bill is the easy-going one of the bunch. "Yer right, Pecos. C'mon, let's git on with the game."

The cards are dealt and Felix, seemingly with beginner's luck, wins. He also wins the next pot. The boys are a little disturbed by this. They deal the next hand.

Felix, seeing that he has been dealt three kings, looks around the table, thinking it best to let them know he is not a novice. "I should tell you hombres that I once won a poker-playing contest back East."

Cisco, looking real serious, says, "Thais alright. We'll just keep hopin' we got a chance." He hides a wink at the others and continues, "Say, you fellers hear what happened t'other night at the Big Bear Saloon in Reedville? Stranger was winnin' most every pot 'til One-Eye Dawson remembered him. He was a riverboat card shark. Sheriff found his body floatin' in the river next mornin'. Guess he was just too lucky fer his own good."

Mad Dog gives Felix a hard look. "All right, fellers, let's see what yer holdin'."

Felix throws his cards on the table face down. "I got nothing. Lousy luck! I hope you hombres will excuse me. I'm right smartly hankerin' to wet mah whistle and grab some grub, pards. Real nice to've met up with you all, ah do believe." He jumps up, leaving his winnings. While the card players watch, smiling slyly, he hurries back to join the other Directors at the bar, again remembering to walk as bowlegged as possible.

Mad Dog marvels. "Well, lookit that! Lookit the way that poor old dude walks. Sumpin' mighty wrong with his laigs. Musta been in a bad accident."

Pecos scratches his head, confused. "What was he talkin' 'bout? Sounded mighty strange to me." He repeats Felix's words, "'Right smartly hankerin' fer some grub.' I do believe the guy's a little loco. Could jist have said straight out that he was hongry." They all nod agreement after raking in Felix's abandoned winnings. Pecos says, "Deal Big Bill." And they continue their game.

The Directors, gathered around the bar, give Felix the once-over. Will Toomey grins at him. "Guess ya taught them thar card mongers a lesson alright, huh, Felix?"

Felix glares at Will. "Sure wanna thank ya fer yer lessons, Will." Then he looks at the bartender, who is obviously amused as well. "Whiskey!" As the bartender pours Felix a stiff one, he asks the others, "'Nother round, gents? What'll it be this time, tequila, Sidewinders, Crazy Horse Gin?"

Just then, Virgil, the burly marksman from the shooting range, shouts drunkenly from the far end of the bar, "Crazy Horse Gin for all! It's on me, gents! I kin see yer after Arizona."

The bartender pours everybody a drink. The Directors hesitate, but their fear of provoking Virgil dominates them, so they raise their glasses to him and gulp the first drink down, then another, and a third. Then they commence to fall in succession, like dominos, flat on their faces on the barroom floor, except for one, Henry. Virgil walks menacingly down the bar, stepping over the prone Directors as he goes, and says mockingly, "Well, now, Killer, you ain't touched your drink. Ain't it strong enough fer you?"

Finding the burly drunk frightening, Henry says, "Oh, yes. I certainly thank you for your well-intended hospitality, sir, but I am a believer in *mens sano in corpore sano.*"

Virgil, long drunk himself, shouts to the bartender, "Willie, you got any of that? That 'men's samo'?"

Willie thinks, then says, "Men's samo? No, never heard of it."

Henry is careful to be polite. "It's not a drink, sir. It is Latin, meaning 'a healthy mind in a healthy body'. The Lord never meant us to abuse our minds and bodies with alcohol."

Virgil looks at the little director in genuine astonishment. Then his expression changes. He grabs Henry, spins him around, propels him through the swinging doors of the bar, and throws him into the horse trough at the front of the hotel. Laughter erupts from deep in his belly as he looks down at his prey. "There, now, drink all you want, Percy. The Lord ain't got nothin' aginst indulgin' in a good drink of water, has He?"

Henry pops up, blindly striking at the drunk. His tiny fist hits the big drunk's chin. Then he falls back, underneath the water. Just then a hand reaches out and whirls the bully around, followed quickly by Jim landing a haymaker on drunken Virgil's jaw. He then falls unconscious to the street. Satisfied, Jim walks quickly back into the barroom, passing Hound Dog Bassett, who has just arrived back in town and has witnessed this fight.

The little director climbs out of the trough and stands over the unconscious bully with amazement. Some of the other Directors, having regained consciousness, come to the barroom door and see Henry standing over his flattened tormenter.

Felix Herkimer is amazed. "He punched his lights out!"

Beamish calls out, "That's enough, Henry! Don't kill him! We got work to do."

Henry proudly steps over Virgil and swaggers in to join the other Directors. Hound Dog follows him back inside.

The Directors treat Henry like a conquering hero, as they all walk over to the bar. Henry is bursting with pride. "Sometimes I get very physical . . . and when I do . . . pow!"

They all toast him. "To Henry! To our guy, Henry!" But they are soon drowned out when the crowd cheers lustily for the piano player, as he goes into the strains of "Pony Boy," and the dancing girls prance out on the stage and go into their high-kicking routine.

This quickly gets Beamish and the mostly drunken Directors' attention. They watch raptly along with the boisterous crowd. Beamish's eye is caught by one very shapely dancer. She glances in his direction seductively as she kicks her legs in the air.

In the audience is a husky young roughneck who is trying to catch her attention too, as he throws kisses to her and claps boisterously. Beamish lights a cigar and, as he rivets his gaze on the girl, the smoke from the cigar gets into his right eye. Beamish blinks his eye and it looks like an inviting wink to the dancing girl. She winks back. Beamish rubs his eye and blinks twice again. The girl again mistakes it for Beamish winking at her, and winks back at Beamish again.

The young roughneck sees all of this. He glowers jealously, stands up, stalks over to Beamish, and grabs him hard by his shirtfront with his left hand. "I seen you gittin' fresh with Charmaine! Winkin' and all. I'm gonna bust you up, dude!" He winds up to land a haymaker with his right hand.

The girls have left the stage to mingle with the customers. Charmaine sees what is happening and hurries towards the adversaries, shouting as she crosses the room, "Zeke! Leave him alone! Don't you dare hit my Uncle Harry!"

Still holding the quaking Beamish, Zeke says, "Yer Uncle Harry, Charmaine?" She joins Zeke and Beamish. "Yes, my dear Uncle Harry."

Zeke releases Beamish. "Geez, Uncle Harry, I'm right sorry. Please excuse me. I thought you was . . ." Zeke gets all bashful and embarrassed.

Beamish—vastly relieved—and knowing what to do, says, "Uh, yes, yes. Uh, Charmaine, honey, is there any place here we can talk privately, and, uh, discuss family affairs?" He gives her a very direct look.

Charmaine flashes a sexy smile at him. "My dressing room. Come along, Uncle Harry."

Jim watches closely as the very exciting Charmaine takes Beamish's arm and walks him down the hall next to the stage to her dressing room. Two of the saloon's tough boys follow discreetly behind them to stand guard.

Chapter 17

Inside Charmaine's dressing room, Albert can't take his eye off of her skimpy outfit. With his best East Coast manners, he says, "Thanks, young lady, very kind of you. Of course, I could have handled the situation myself, but I appreciate your good intentions."

Charmaine lays it on thick. "Of course, a big, strong, experienced man like you knows how to handle anything. But after all, you *were* winking and flirting with me. What did you have in mind, hon?"

Beamish is quite serious about what actually happened. "Well, smoke got in my eyes."

She is seductive. "That's a beautiful way to put it! Blinded by instant attraction. I seen you and smoke kinda got in my eyes, too, honey." She tilts her head up and comes close to him.

Looking down at her and still oblivious of the direction she's headed, he whiffs her perfume. "When the smoke got in my eyes . . ."

Charmaine purrs, "It was love at first sight, right?"

Now Beamish sees where she's going, and doesn't really want to play her game. "I'd better be getting back to my colleagues."

Charmaine places her hand on his arm, not wanting to lose her prize. "You're kinda the leader of the Director fellers, ain't you? Them fellers that come out to stake the gold claim?"

Now becoming incredulous, he blurts out, "Gold? No, no, we're not here for any gold. Who in the world started that rumor, as a matter of fact? We're after Arizona Adams and his gang."

Charmaine looks wise and very skeptical. "Sure, I know. There's no gold." Now she winks. "Why don't we have a cozy little drink or two while we chat, Mr. . . . .?"

"Beamish, Albert Beamish."

Charmaine smiles at him seductively. "Howdy, Al." Then she pulls a bottle from a shelf and pours drinks for herself and Beamish in large tumblers and hands him one.

"Next show don't go on for two hours. So we can relax and you can tell Charmaine all about it. Anybody in Whistle Stop will tell you that you can trust Charmaine with your life." She raises her glass to him, a bit roguishly. "Down the hatch and a roll in the grass, Al."

Still a bit drunk from that last round at the bar, Beamish just takes a small sip and almost gags. "Strong stuff!"

"Hey, strong drink for a manly man! Down it, honey!

Feeling he must rise to her compliment, Beamish throws his head back to gulp the drink down, while Charmaine quickly dumps most of her drink into the flower pot next to her chair. As they take more drinks, she repeats this manoeuver, making small talk, until Beamish is again completely soused. He reaches for her hand and becomes amorous.

"Oh! You like Charmaine, honey?"

"You bet! Gimmee a kiss. I like your golden hair, sweetie." He reaches for her golden locks.

She catches his hand before it gets to her hair. "It matches the gold you're here for, don't it? You kin tell me the truth, Al, not that Arizona Adams cover-up bull. No one in their right mind would go against him."

"Only you are on my mind." He kisses her hand.

"Wait just a sec, hon, while I change." Charmaine slips behind a floor screen and slings something over the top of the screen that looks like a very padded brassiere. She emerges looking curiously flat-chested, and dressed only in her camisole and lacy drawers. Beamish, drunk as he is, looks startled at the change. Nevertheless, he lurches towards her and tries again to give her a drunken kiss. In doing so, he knocks off her blonde wig, revealing short, dark, frizzed hair.

Totally drunk, Beamish is confused. "Where's Charmaine? Where's the girl I came here with?"

Charmaine turns her back and bends over to pick up the wig, when suddenly Beamish collapses on her back and they both end up in a heap on the floor. Charmaine rolls Beamish's body off her, and quickly searches his wallet and his pockets.

"Damn! No map!" She takes a few bills he won't miss, then goes to the hall door and beckons to the two toughs, shaking her head negatively. "Dump him in the alley, boys. The only gold he has is in his teeth."

The toughs drag Beamish into the alley and deposit him on top of a garbage barrel. He raises his head a bit, then passes out cold. As the toughs go into the back door of the saloon, Jim appears in the saloon alley, looks both ways, then half drags Beamish down the alley back to the hotel entrance, saying under his breath, "You're damn lucky I have to tolerate you until we finish our business, you bastard."

Chapter 18

The next morning Jim and the Directors, all showing signs of being hung over, meet up in the town square, which is filled with the town's people chatting and yapping, all still wondering what these scheming New Yorkers are really doing there. A line of horses is hitched up, with each Director standing in front of his horse.

Hound Dog Bassett is already sitting on his hired horse, trying to blend in, watching the goings on.

Jim scans the entire sight for a moment, takes a long, deep breath, then addresses the Directors. "We've got a long way to go, men. The time for a showdown with Arizona Adams has come. We're gonna ride out to the Curtain Lines tracks where the Adams Gang usually attacks the trains and see if we can pick up their trail. We'll let this town know what we're made of! Right?"

They all respond together with bravado. "Yeh!" "Right!" "You bet!" "We'll sure show 'em!"

While Jim is talking, the young town mischief-maker, Tommy, looks around, then stealthily pushes a small cactus under the saddle of Beamish's horse.

Jim shouts a loud war whoop, "Yaaah ho! Mount up!" Some Directors have obviously been on a horse before, while others fall off a few times before they are settled in their saddles.

The gathered crowd cheers as Jim and the Directors start riding out. Jim gallops ahead, with the Directors following very awkwardly after him, trailed by Hound Dog Bassett, but not for long. As soon as Beamish starts to gallop, his horse is stuck by the cactus and rears up in the air, sending him flying, and then stampedes right into the other horses and riders. Those Directors that are new to riding fall off like tenpins going down. Felix Herkimer's horse heads at a panicky gallop for the clump of trees ringing the town square, and Felix soon gets knocked off by a low tree limb. Hound Dog Bassett's horse gallops in the opposite direction toward his barn, with Hound Dog holding on for dear life.

The crowd joins in with the prankster, Tommy, who is laughing and whooping with delight at the greenhorn Directors. Jim, who is out ahead and has not witnessed the chaos behind him, turns and sees Beamish, Felix, and several other Directors rolling on the ground, and the rest—still on their horses—galloping in different directions. Trying to keep from laughing along with the crowd, Jim turns his horse around, rides back to the hotel and waits, as one limping, bedraggled director after another comes dolefully back. Shaking his head at the prime object of his general disdain, he says, "Well, Beamish, I guess Arizona Adams can rest easy for another day. This hunt is adjourned until we've taken a few practice rides. You all are at your leisure."

*

Later, as Jim heads towards the *Gazette* office, an old prospector walks toward him, leading his horse with a dead man draped over its back. As they pass, Jim sees that the dead man is Sage, his only confidant in the gang. Feeling very sad, because Sage was his father's former wrangler whom he knew since he was a boy, he whispers to himself, "Damn that scum, Grady. He'll pay for this in spades." Jim watches with a heavy heart as the prospector walks on toward the sheriff's office, then he turns and continues on to the *Gazette*.

Jim enters the *Gazette* office deep in serious thought. Ellen is busy at the typewriter. "Well, well, well, if it isn't the man of the hour. Really, Jim, your gang of fearless fogies can't even sit on a standing horse. Give it up. It's hopeless."

He gives her a sad but coy look. "It may be hopeless, Ellen, but I can't forget that these outlaws are vermin. I've been pacing around the back pasture for the past two hours trying to think of something."

"Stop thinking. Just ship the Directors back to New York and stop trying to kill yourself."

He snaps to attention. "Kill myself?" Then he realizes she's just using an expression. "Yes, literally, if I keep trying to work with these dudes. But don't worry, Ellen, I actually thought of a plan." He calls to Charlie in the printing plant, "Can you come in here a minute?"

Charlie cuts off his press and joins them in the office.

"Soon as I dictate this story to Ellen, I want you to run it right off, Charlie."

"Sure, boss."

Jim dictates, "Headline in 32-point bold type across the entire width of the front page: 'GOLD SHIPMENT DUE TO PASS THROUGH WHISTLE STOP FRIDAY MORNING.' Followed by the body copy: 'The Curtain Rail Lines will be carrying a large payroll shipment of gold, bound for a copper mine near Tucson, Arizona. It is being routed through Whistle Stop on Friday morning at 11 A.M. to take on water for the engine. Three special guards will be aboard the train'."

Completing her notes, Ellen looks up. "Is that true?"

Jim looks directly at her. "No. But the Adams Gang won't know that. They'd never resist that bait, but it'll take some preparing to get it right. Charlie, set the type and run the edition. Be sure that a good supply of the papers get to Reedville and Lincoln Gap by this afternoon."

"Sure boss."

"I'll see you later, beautiful." He gives Ellen a peck on the cheek and leaves the *Gazette* office.

Chapter 19

A short time later, Jim is in Beamish's hotel room conducting business, never once bringing up the Charmaine incident, or the Directors' failures at the shooting range and riding out to track the gang. "So that's the plan. Do you think you can order a cancellation of all trains after 11 A.M.?"

Beamish starts to pace. "That's a tough order unless it's a very big emergency. When?"

"Friday. And this is it, Al, because baiting this trap is the only way."

Trying his best to maintain his authority—when the unmentioned facts of their failures hang heavy in the room—Beamish shows guarded respect that Jim has come up with a decent plan. "Seems like it just might work. I'll send Cavendish an urgent wireless with my instructions. I only hope you know what you're doing."

"Good. Tell him to let the 11 A.M. arrive on schedule. Better hold up the rest until Saturday morning."

Never really trusting Jim, Beamish now expresses his worst fear. "You don't mind if I risk my neck, do you, Courtney?"

"Your neck and mine too, Albert. I'm going to head over to the sheriff's office and get him and the mayor on board with the plan. I'll catch up with you later to go over the fine details."

*

Jim and Mayor Kibbee are sitting in front of the sheriff's desk, which has nothing on it but an inkwell and pen. Mayor Kibbee is looking mighty skeptical. "You're askin' a lot, Jim."

Jim is dead serious. "But desperate measures are called for. I'm betting that newspaper story will lure them into an attack on the train. Then my men will engage them in a gunfight from the train windows, and . . ."

The mayor cuts in with a laugh in his voice, "Your men! Them fancypants from New York?"

"Well, I get your point, but nobody else around here will face Arizona and his gang. Maybe these fellows aren't handy with a gun, but at least they're willing to try—and so am I! And we've got to go after the Adams Gang and show them they can't get away with blowing a safe and shooting two people like they did on their last job. Otherwise, we'll have no one to blame but our own fool selves, if the gang's next job is robbin' the Whistle Stop Bank and shootin' up our citizens. Do you want that?"

Kibbee considers Jim's points, takes a gander at Sheriff Lynch, who is looking down while he plays with his cell keys, filled with shame that he has been useless against Arizona. Disgusted that he has to put up with Lynch, the mayor looks at Jim with his full respect. "All right, given that we got them Directors to help, I guess we have to gamble on it."

Jim gives the mayor a slight nod of understanding, and then talks to Lynch, who looks up with a start. "Sheriff, when the train arrives here at eleven Friday morning, you will order all the passengers off, telling them it has to be side-tracked for repairs, and will be ready to roll again on Saturday morning. Meanwhile, arrange for them to stay at the Assay Hotel at no cost to them."

"Yup. Free lodgins and all the dust they can swallow." He takes a stab at a joke.

Jim is not laughing. "You also need to tell the engineer, the fireman, and the conductors they'll be put up, too. We don't want anybody hurt who doesn't belong in a gunfight, if they can be replaced. You got that?" The sheriff nods.

Satisfied, Jim asks, "Can we get replacements, Mayor Kibbee?"

"Got some good retired railroaders in town. Fred Decker can engineer the train and Bert Dermott can stoke her. They're tough men, too. Been on posses in the past."

"Good. Let's get to work. Friday's just two days from now."

Chapter 20

Late that afternoon, in the town of Reedville, Grady Profit rides up to the general store, dismounts, and hitches his horse to a post in front of the store. The sign hanging over the door says "Nothing In Particular, Everything In General." Grady enters and barks, "Coupla sacks of Bull Durham."

The proprietor sees the scruffy and mean-looking Grady, and is immediately nervous. "Yessir." He removes two, white, muslin sacks off the shelf and hands them to Grady, who pockets them and drops a dime on the counter. He is about to leave when he spots a pile of *Whistle Stop Gazettes* at the end of the counter. Grady's eyes widen as he notes the headline:

**GOLD SHIPMENT DUE TO PASS THROUGH
WHISTLE STOP FRIDAY MORNING**

He takes a paper, stops and reads the story, throws a few bits down for the paper, and hightails it out the door. Grady mounts in a hurry and rides back toward the hideout.

*

That night, Bassett, wearing a black mask, moves stealthily toward the back of the *Whistle Stop Gazette* office. Arriving before a window, he looks around to make sure he's alone, then takes a small roll of mechanics tape from his pocket and criss-crosses some of the tape on the window. He then hits the pane with the heel of his hand until the glass falls in, without a sound. Reaching in, he unlocks the window, raises it, and with some effort hauls himself into the office. When Bassett falls inside, he shoots his flickering flashlight beam all around to see the layout, then finds his way into Jim's office, where he begins searching the desk drawers and going through Jim's papers.

Meanwhile, a second figure approaches the same window, which is now wide open. He puts on a black mask, takes a look around and climbs in, unaware that Bassett is already there. He too gets the layout of the place first with his flashlight, then tiptoes towards Jim's office, his flashlight flickering.

Just as the second man heads towards Jim's office, Bassett gets up and goes into the printing plant. The second man also goes through Jim's desk drawers and papers, then he, too, heads for the printing plant. They both search for some evidence of illegal activity on Jim's part that will throw out his claim to the Curtain Rail Lines. Inevitably, the beams from their flashlights cross like sword blades, and each is suddenly aware of the presence of the other.

Their flickering flashlight beams indicate hysterical movements before going out, as each tries in a panic to escape from the other. Both turn and run for the open window. They crash into one another and fall to the floor, where they thrash around trying to break loose. One finally does, and tries to climb out of the window, but as he does so, the sleuth still on the floor grabs wildly at his pant legs and pulls hard. With his pants now around his ankles, he kicks at the sleuth on the floor, and at last manages to tumble out of the window onto the ground.

He rises and tries to run. Hobbled by his pants, he pulls them up and yanks off his mask. It is Bassett. He scurries down Main Street toward the Assay Hotel. A little stray dog that had been snoozing wakes up and takes off after him, yapping wildly and jumping up on him as he runs. Bassett flies into the lobby of the Assay Hotel. Luke, the clerk, who has been sleeping, with his chair tilted against the wall behind the counter, wakes up as his chair falls. He sees Bassett trying to look cool as he walks toward the stairway. But the excited little dog is right behind Bassett.

"Hey, mister, no dogs ain't allowed in here."

Bassett looks around. "It's not my dog."

"You sure? He kinda has a resemblance to you."

Bassett shoos the little dog out of the lobby into the street and goes quickly up the stairway, while Luke resumes sitting in his chair and again starts nodding.

Back on Main Street, the little dog starts to go back up the street, but spots the second man. It is Albert Beamish running toward the hotel. The little dog takes up the game again, running beside Beamish, yapping wildly and jumping up on him. Beamish has stuffed his mask hurriedly in his pants pocket, and it falls out. The little dog picks it up and follows him into the hotel. In the lobby, the little dog sits up in a begging position, holding the mask in its mouth. Panting and completely flustered, Beamish tries to grab the mask before Luke wakes up. But Luke again falls off his chair and, rising, sees Beamish and the little dog.

"What in hell is goin' on here? I tole that other fella and ahm tellin' you, no dogs ain't allowed here! What's he got in his mouth?"

Beamish condescendingly says to Luke, "I don't know. I never saw him before," and then to the little dog, "Get out! Go! Go!" But the dog stays put.

Luke is looking at the mask. "What is that thing in his mouth?"

Beamish improvises, "It's his collar. It came loose. Here little doggie, let me fix it." He snatches the mask from the dog, who tugs at it playfully. Beamish yanks it free, and tries to wrap it around the dog's neck, but only manages to put it on his head. The dog runs out of the lobby with the mask on his head, just as one of the little, old ladies lodging at the hotel is coming in. She sees the mask.

"Stop, thief! Stop!"

But the little dog disappears up the street. Beamish tips his hat to the lady, rushes up the stairway and into his room, where he falls into the chair, panting and completely defeated.

*

The next morning in the *Whistle Stop Gazette* office, Sheriff Lynch is watching Jim and Ellen look through the papers that are strewn all over the floor. "You say nothin' is missin'?"

Jim looks up at the sheriff. "Nothing."

Ellen jokes, "Maybe two boxes of those new fangled rubber bands, which were darn hard to order and get shipped here from the East Coast."

Sheriff Lynch takes a battered notebook and the stub of a pencil out of his hip pocket, and wetting the end of the pencil, begins to write laboriously. "Two boxes of rubber—how yuh spell rubber? R-u-b-e-r, right?"

She's deadpan. "Near enough."

Jim says, sardonically, "You think we ought to offer a reward for any information about this, sheriff?"

The sheriff, not getting his meaning, says, "You kin depend on me, Jim. I'll be after the coyotes. Rest easy." He leaves looking intently at his notebook.

They watch him go, then break out in big smiles. Ellen says, "There's one thing you can depend on, Jim. With Sheriff Lynch on their trail, the robbers have nothing to worry about."

"I think this break-in is strange, but since we never lock up . . . it was probably one of the vagrants looking for a bottle. What I'm worried about is tomorrow."

Ellen looks at Jim, very worried about that too, but doesn't comment.

Chapter 21

At the Whistle Stop train station the next morning, Mayor Kibbee and Sheriff Lynch wait as the morning train chugs to a stop. The conductor helps the Whistle Stop passengers off the train. Then the mayor and sheriff climb aboard, as Jim, the Directors, and the experienced train men, Fred Decker and Burt Dermott, watch from their hiding place behind the station.

Inside the train car, Sheriff Lynch addresses the passengers. "Folks, we're sure sorry tuh cause y'all any inconvenience, but this here train has tuh be taken out of service fer repairs."

The passengers register confusion, frustration, and anger.

A cowboy yells out, "Whatta ya mean?"

A well-dressed Eastern woman says, "I have family waiting for me!"

A businessman complains, "Hey, I got to be on my way, I got business in Tucson."

Sheriff Lynch holds up his hands trying to calm them down. "Well, sorry agin, but the engineer cain't let y'all continue without this work being done. But y'all are gittin' free rooms fer the day and tonight at the Assay Hotel. Jes pile your luggage on that thar wagon we've provided, and follow the mayor and myself to the hotel." Grumblingly, the passengers take their possessions and disembark, along with the conductors and engineers.

When the train is empty, Fred and Bert climb into the engine cab, as Jim and the Directors board the first passenger car from the opposite side of the train. The Directors are so scared that they all jump when they hear the train whistle let out a test blast.

Then, carefully looking both ways to insure he is not observed, none other than Hound Dog Bassett surreptitiously hops aboard the last passenger car, just as the train starts with a lurch. He walks through to the Directors car, observes that Jim is busy arranging each of the well-armed Directors at a window, and slips into the washroom.

The wheels are moving fast now, as the train travels through the flatlands a few miles from Whistle Stop. The Directors are at their windows, holding either a six-shooter or a rifle, scanning the prairie apprehensively. The land seems quiet and peaceful, then something moves in the distance.

Jim is steady as he calls out, "Get ready, men! Something's moving over there."

The Directors are panicky and begin yelling out.

"What's moving?"

"Where?"

"Oh my God!"

Jim is looking out of the window, pointing. "Behind that clump of bushes! Take aim. Don't fire until we're in the fifty-yard range."

Bassett, hearing this, sticks his head out of the wash room door, sees them all pointing their guns, and then quickly ducks in again.

Jim calls out, "Seventy yards . . . sixty . . . fifty." He turns and looks around, about to yell "fire," and does an incredulous double-take. The car appears to be empty. He's astounded. "What the devil?" A slight movement catches Jim's eye. He notices the heel of a shoe sticking out from between two train seats, then another, and another. Shaking his head in disbelief, Jim looks out the window again, scanning the desert brush. "All clear, boys! Just a stray cow." Slowly, Beamish, Herkimer, Toomey, Travis and the rest of the Directors cautiously emerge from between the seats.

Jim can't help making fun at their expense. "Well, now, that was a very clever bit of strategy for all of you deputy sheriffs. Very tricky! You were just setting up an ambush, right?" The Directors emerge sheepishly, and reluctantly take their posts at the windows again. The train rolls on.

Henry Travis, very relieved, says with bravado, "It's a wild goose chase. I think they know we're after them, and I bet they're scared. They won't show up. So, Mr. Courtney, why don't we just go back to Whistle Stop?"

Jim says confidently, "They'll show, Mr. Travis. Keep your eyes peeled and your guns ready."

The young director Dilbert Findley's chubby hand is shaking. "I agree, it's a waste of time. I vote we go back."

Jim surveys the looks on the Directors' faces and sees scared rabbits. All of them, including Beamish. "If you're set on returning, I'll pull the emergency cord and the engineer will stop the train. Those of you who want to can walk back to town—it's only about twenty miles. You should be able to make it by two or three in the morning, although there's some pretty rough country to cover. Unless, of course, you're delayed by snakes or a long swim across the river.

The Directors, now beyond fear, all yell out at the same time.

"Oh my God, snakes!"

"I can't swim."

"We'll die out there of hunger and thirst."

"We're gonna die anyway from the Adams Gang's bullets."

Beamish jumps in, suddenly apprehensive, but with the most at stake, "Well, now, just a minute. There are things to be considered here. I'm just as anxious as anyone else to deal with these outlaws, but I suggest that we act like businessmen and put the matter to a vote."

The cowardly Directors act unanimously. "Aye! Aye!"

Beamish calls out, "Those in favor of going back to Whistle Stop raise your hands." All of the Directors' hands shoot up. But, just as they do so, shots ring out across the prairie, and horsemen come racing towards the train.

Jim jumps into action. "One shot's worth a dozen votes. Man your posts! Hold your fire until I give the order." He looks out of the window and sees that the gang is coming on fast, firing and shouting, led by Grady Profit, who—just as Jim expected—is dressed in black, posing as Arizona Adams. Jim has been waiting for this moment, knowing he wants to put his first bullet right through Grady's heart. "Hold! Hold!—Now! Fire!" The Directors fire their guns wildly.

The door to the rest room at the rear end of the car opens just wide enough for Bassett to stick his head out and see what is taking place. A volley of bullets from Grady's bunch sprays holes in the windows. Bassett quickly shuts the door and locks it. While listening to the shooting and wild yelling, he wipes his sweating forehead with his handkerchief, takes a seat on the commode, and waits fearfully to see which way the firefight is going to go.

Two directors, armed with high-powered rifles, fire and fly backwards from the recoil, ending up draped over the arms of seats on the opposite side of the car.

Jim aims at Grady and shoots. He sees Hogan, who was riding next to the masquerading Grady, fall from his horse. Jim whispers to himself, "Damn, I've got to get him." The rest of the Directors' furious fusillade does not hit one other outlaw.

Out on the plain, the gang comes to a halt and circles Grady. He says, "What the hell were they shootin' at? Hogan's the only one that got clipped. But there's one helluva lot of guns on that train! Ain't seen that before. Corky, you and Jack ride ahead, takin' the short-cut to the tracks after the curve, and do the body-on-the-tracks trick. That'll stop the train. Then we'll board her, handle these guards, and get that gold!"

Corky and Jack gallop at full speed through a shortcut in the rocks to a spot up ahead, where a curve in the track conceals them from the sight of the engineer. They quickly beat off their horses with their hats and lie down across the tracks.

Back inside the train car, Jim is hanging his head out of the window. Just as the train comes out of the curve, he can see Corky and Jack laying on the tracks in the distance. He says to himself, "Aw shucks, that skunk Grady's using my bodies-on-the-tracks trick. Gotta stop this." Jim runs through the passenger car door and climbs across to the engine cab.

In the cab, Fred, the engineer, has already spotted the "bodies," and is sounding the whistle urgently as the train rushes toward them. Jim enters the cab. Fred frantically says, "Jim, there's two bodies . . . !"

Jim screams at him over the noise of the engine, "Don't brake, keep going!"

Fred can't believe it. "What? But we'll kill 'em if . . ."

Jim jumps in as they are closing in on the bodies. "Do it!"

Fred reluctantly keeps the train rolling right on. When the train is almost upon the bodies, they suddenly come to life and roll frantically off the tracks. The outlaws flee to their horses and hightail it back to join the gang.

Grady is dumbfounded. "Never even slowed down! How'd they know Corky and Jack wasn't daid? That trick always worked for Arizona. Well, we'll get them at the spur. Let's go." They gallop toward the rail spur.

On the train, Jim leaps from the engine car back to the passenger car, throws open the door, and barks orders to the Directors, "Listen up men! As they've done before, they're heading for the rail spur up ahead where the switch is. They aim to shunt us off onto the side track so they can board us. If we get stopped there, it's all over for us! Here's what we gotta do. When we're about fifty yards from the switch, fire away at it on my command. Keep firing at the switch and don't let up no matter what. Forget about firing at the gang. We're closing in. Get to your posts!"

The Directors all scurry to their posts, poise their guns and rifles out of the windows, and wait for Jim's command.

Grady and the gang are riding hard on the spur track, racing for the switch.

When the train is fifty yards away, Jim yells, "Fire!" The men all let loose a volley at the switch. Jim barks, "Keep firing! Keep firing!"

Bullets spray off the spur switch continually. Suddenly Grady and the gang pull up short and stop. The train whizzes by on the main tracks. Grady is hopping mad. "They knew it again! Damn it, we got to git men aboard that train! Rush it and git aboard any way you can. Let's go!" They gallop off, closing the gap between themselves and the train, shooting as they go.

Jim sees this from the passenger car window, assesses their odds, races back across to the engine cab, and holds onto Fred the engineer's shoulder. "Do ya know where the oil can is?"

Fred nods. "In the tool box there."

He gives Fred a pat, pulls open the tool box, takes out the oil can, and dashes back toward the engine cab door.

Grady and the gang are riding full gallop toward the train, their guns blasting away.

With bullets flying by him, Jim straddles the coupling-pin connecting the engine cab and the passenger car, and pours a gush of oil on the pin. Ducking bullets, Jim jumps through the engine car door and squats to put the oil can back in the box. Just then Fred screams, clutches at his heavily bleeding left shoulder, and topples from his seat.

Bert yells out, "Fred's hurt! We're running wild!"

Jim grabs a towel hanging on the cab wall and tosses it to Bert. "Make a tourniquet. He's losing a lot of blood." Bert kneels beside Fred and makes the tourniquet.

Jim quickly takes Fred's seat at the train controls. "Fred, can you hear me?"

Fred answers weakly, "Yeh."

Jim glances down for a split second. "Try to hold on, Fred. Help me to run this train."

Fred gasps in pain. "The big lever to your left. Pull it all the way down to stop."

Jim's adamant. "We're not stopping. They'll kill us all. We've got to keep going."

Fred nods slightly. "Watch the boiler gauge. Don't get over 175 degrees or she'll blow."

Jim asks, "The whistle control?"

"The cord right over your head."

"The steam jet?"

"Second lever to your left on the control panel." Then Fred's head falls to the side. He is unconscious.

Bert listens to his breath. "Fred's passed out! He can't help us no more."

Jim keeps the train rolling. He looks out the window and sees Gyp and two other outlaws he does not recognize reaching for the handrail of the last car. Gyp levers himself aboard and begins climbing to the roof of the train. The two others follow. Jim pushes the big lever on the left up to get the train to run at top speed.

Bert yells out, "Jim, slow it down! That's Suicide Curve up ahead. At this speed we'll derail!" Jim makes no move to slow the train. Bert is frantic. "Slow down, fer God's sake! Pull the control lever. We're almost at the curve!"

Jim settles in. "No! Better to risk the curve than end up in the hands of this gang!"

Bert knows the truth. "God save us, we'll crash!"

The train reaches the beginning of Suicide Curve and starts to sway. The outlaws already on the top of the train struggle to stay on their feet. On one side of Suicide Curve there is a bridge over Apache Lake river valley. As the train gathers speed over the bridge, it starts to sway wildly. Grady and the other outlaws have to drop back, no longer able to mount the rear of the train.

Meanwhile, in the rest room, Hound Dog Bassett is thrown from wall to wall. He clutches at the full washbowl, which dumps water all over him, then at the community towel attached to the wall, and swings over to the open toilet, which he ends up sitting on and falls in. He rises, now wet, and is thrown against the stack of rough toilet paper. He falls and, as he rolls on the floor, the little squares of paper adhere to his wet face and suit, so that he looks very much like a dirty snowman.

The train is swaying dangerously, near to capsizing, as it charges across the bridge. The two new outlaws fall off, in a long descent to the water below. Gyp goes flat on the roof and hangs on desperately.

Grady and the rest of the gang now follow a roundabout ground route, to ford the river, in hot pursuit.

Jim manages to keep the train from derailing, by slowing it down a bit as it rounds the final part of Suicide Curve and heads out across the flatlands again.

The outlaw Gyp, still on top of the train, stands up, races forward over the passenger car, and, drawing his gun, climbs down to the platform of the engine cab and enters. He levels his gun at Jim and Bert. "Stop this train—now!"

Jim, keeping his head turned away from Gyp by looking out of the window, slows the train and brings it to a stop.

Gyp gives orders to Jim. "Git over here by this dude." He gestures with his gun towards Bert. Jim, still shielding his face from Gyp, knowing that he'll recognize him, sidles over to Bert, and sees that his shovel is half inside the boiler, filled with flaming coals. Just then Gyp gets a partial, side view, look at Jim. "Hey, ain't you . . . ?"

Jim suddenly grabs the shovel handle and throws the flaming coals into Gyp's face. Blinded, he screams in pain. Jim then jumps him, easily wrests his gun away, shoves him out of the cab door, and throws him off the engine platform to the ground, where he writhes in pain.

Jim quickly occupies the engineer's seat once again and gets the train moving. But the delay has allowed Grady and the gang to close in on the train. Two other new outlaws Grady has added to the gang for this job gallop up parallel to the engine and level their guns right at Jim. Jim quickly grabs the overhead cord and a powerful jet of steam engulfs the gunmen. Their horses squeal and gallop off at full speed. But now Corky and Jack gallop up to the engine car. They leap from their horses to the platform, between the passenger car and the engine cab, and tug with all their strength on the coupling-pin between the cab and the engine, with the intention of separating the engine from the passenger cars. Unaware that the coupling-pin was heavily oiled by Jim to guard against this exact action—which he had done when he led the Adams Gang— they tug mightily, and suddenly both go flying off the train as it goes racing on, still coupled.

Back in the passenger car, the Directors are all pulling themselves back to their feet after Suicide Curve. Felix Herkimer looks out the window. "They're still coming!"

Henry Travis yells out, "We're running out of time!"

Beamish exclaims, "We're running out of bullets, too!"

Felix Herkimer is very worried. "Maybe we should all keep one last bullet!"

Beamish is puzzled. "What for?"

Felix is philosophical. "For ourselves. It's better than falling into the hands of these murdering thugs! They'll shoot us down like dogs!"

With that, all of the other Directors are filled with fear.

"Oh my God!"

"Lord help us!"

"Save me!"

One falls to his knees and starts praying.

Henry Travis tries to be logical. "Maybe if we just surrender . . ."

Beamish warns them, "Forget that. Make no mistake, they're murderers. They won't take prisoners!" The train whistle sounds frantically now. The gang is again closing in.

Having considered the options, Felix says with strong conviction, "They can have anything I've got. Maybe they'll stop trying to board the train." With that, he strips off his gold watch, his rings, and takes all the cash from his bulging wallet. The others hesitate, but then follow his lead. They toss everything out the windows.

The gang, seeing all the money and jewelry flying out the windows, stop, dismount, spread out, and very quickly gather up the loot.

Jim watches this with disbelief, then asks Bert, "How much farther to Lincoln Gap?"

Bert, still tending to Fred, looks up. "Just around the bend. Coupla minutes now."

Jim keeps the train racing along at full speed, with the whistle frantically screaming.

A crowd of people have gathered at the Lincoln Gap station on the outskirts of town. They see the train round the bend and head toward the station. A man in the crowd yells out, "That train's being attacked!"

Another Lincoln Gap man agrees. "It has to be them Adams cutthroats!"

A third is full of defiance. "C'mon! Let's get them murderin' crooks!" Many of the men in the crowd mount their horses and race out to engage the outlaws.

The outlaws, scooping up the remaining loot on the ground, see the posse heading for them from the distance. They jump on their horses and gallop off. The townspeople ride in pursuit.

Another group of Lincoln Gap people run up to the train as it comes to a stop. Jim yells out of the engine cab, "We've got a badly wounded man up here. He's got to get to a doc right away. Give me a hand to get him down." Two of the men in the crowd help Jim to lower Fred out of the cab and drape him over a horse. They ride off with him to the doc's office.

Satisfied that Fred will get help, Jim looks around at the gathered crowd. "We're sure glad to meet you folks. We'd be mighty grateful if you would be kind enough to escort us into your town."

Bert is standing next to Jim, and by his manner shows him a lot of respect. "There's a workin' spur about twenty minutes up the track. I can handle sidetrackin' the train on it and then I'll git right back and meet you in town."

Jim shakes his hand. "You're a good man, Bert. See ya in a while, then, and thanks."

The townspeople help Jim and the Directors onto their horses or buckboards, and they all ride back into Lincoln Gap town. Still covered in little bits of paper, the incredulous Hound Dog waits a few minutes, then follows them discreetly on foot.

Jim says to his riding partner, "We'll have to catch an east bound train back to Whistle Stop."

The man has news. "Not today. No trains scheduled for today."

Jim sighs, remembering that all trains have been halted. "That figures."

The man says, "Don't worry, I kin rent you my wagon and a coupla horses."

"Thank you, kind sir. We won't be passin' up that offer."

Later on, the tired, depleted, and defeated Directors and Jim ride out of Lincoln Gap in an open-topped, rickety, old wagon drawn by two horses.

Following them, about a quarter of a mile back, is Hound Dog Bassett, on a mule that slows down and stops after twenty paces.

Chapter 22

Early on Saturday morning, Ellen is busy at her typewriter, working on the story about the Curtain Rail Lines Directors' gun battle with the Adams Gang for the next edition of the *Gazette*, when Jim strides in. "We got all the stranded passengers on the 8:10 train. It's a shame we had to interrupt their trips. And we gained exactly nothing by it anyway."

"You're all very lucky you're still alive."

He gives Ellen a look that says, "Let's not discuss it."

She reads aloud as she continues to type the story. "The Curtain Rail Lines passengers continued their westward bound trip on the 8:10 train. The Directors and their fearless leader, James Courtney, Jr.—who says 'We gained exactly nothing' by using this strategy to kill or capture Arizona Adams—consider themselves lucky to be alive." She looks up at him with a big, satisfied smile.

"We're not printing that!"

"Why not? It's the truth!" Not really intending to use it, she pulls the bogus page out of her typewriter, inserts a fresh sheet, and finishes the story.

Frustrated by the truth of the previous day's confrontation, and already thinking about what he must do next, Jim watches her type for a moment, then switches to the subject that has been on his mind. "How's your dad?"

Pulling the completed story from the typewriter, she's obviously concerned. "Not good. He's literally worrying himself to death about the mortgage payment that's coming up. I'm scared, Jim. You were right. If we lose the ranch, and all of our cattle . . ."

"When's the payment due?"

"One week from today."

He looks at her tenderly. "Relax. A lot can happen in a week. And speaking of relaxing, the Corey's are giving a barn dance tomorrow night. I'd be right honored, Miss Ellen, if y'all would consent to being my dancing partner for the evening."

She's obviously happy for the diversion. "Well, you all talked me into accepting. You devil!"

*

The next night, Mr. and Mrs. Corey welcome most of Whistle Stop's townspeople to the hoedown at their big, old barn on the edge of town. Jim and Ellen, who looks beautiful in her light blue dress, enter the festively decorated room. They're delighted to see the best fiddlers and banjo players from miles around set up on the stage, along with jug and washboard musicians, who are all whooping it up and playing with lots of good-old, down-home exuberance. Jim says, "Shall we, darlin'?" Ellen takes his arm and they join the dancers.

Hound Dog Bassett lingers in the corner with some of the other hotel guests. At the continued urging of some of the town matrons, Beamish and the other Directors were corralled into attending the hoedown too. Lined up along the side of the stage, they resist several attempts by town matrons and young ladies to make them join the dancers, but finally they're practically dragged onto the dance floor, and awkwardly join in a fast Zydeco number.

Jim whirls Ellen around the floor, loving the freedom of the dancing and the high spirit it brings. After five straight dances, Ellen is danced out. "I need a breather, Jim."

He could obviously keep going. "All right, come on, grandma."

They slip out a side door and stroll around behind the barn. They're silent for a while, just taking in the full moon and the beauty of the prairie beyond. Jim puts his arm around her and looks in her eyes with deep love. "I sure like the way the moonlight puts silver pearls in your hair. Can I be arrested for stealing a kiss?" He pulls her to him and kisses her, but Ellen pulls back.

"I'll bet you used that line on all the high-style New York women in their fancy Edwardian dresses."

"Yep, and they all fell for it, too. But I told them it would break your heart if you ever lost me, so . . ."

"So you remained faithful to me. Isn't that lucky for me! Well, alright, here's your reward, Romeo." She embraces Jim and they kiss passionately.

"Wow! Now that took my breath away, fair lady. You really stir me . . . well, what I mean is we best set that wedding date, Miss Ellen, and real soon, or . . ."

"Hush, Jim boy, you know I'm sure dreaming of that day too." She laughs enchantingly, then their lips meet again and they kiss deeply. After a while, arm-in-arm, they return to the dance.

Just as Jim and Ellen rejoin the dancers, the town prankster, Tommy, who has been acting silly doing a little jig, falls on the floor with the sole purpose of tripping one of the dumb, old directors. Felix Herkimer, dancing stiffly with one of the town matrons, goes flying onto the dance floor. Other whirling dancers, unable to stop their momentum quickly enough, also trip and fall over them, piling up on one another. Jim and Ellen end up on top of the heap of struggling dancers, which includes most of the disgruntled Directors.

Jim, chuckling at the sight of them, helps Ellen to her feet, quipping, "This looks more like a fall down than a hoedown." As Jim helps other fallen dancers to their feet, he gives Tommy a strong look. The culprit—acting innocent but fooling no one—slinks away, trying very hard to contain his laughter. The musicians strike up the band again. Jim holds his hand out to Ellen. "May I have the pleasure?"

"If you call scraped shins a pleasure. Someone ought to teach that little imp a lesson."

"Tommy knows one pile-up per hoedown is just part of the fun, honey." She laughs with love in her eyes and they join the other couples who have resumed dancing.

*

Later that evening Jim and Ellen are on Jim's buckboard riding out to the ranch. "I admit we were lucky to get out of that with no broken bones," he comments.

"But it sure was just the kind of fun we needed, with everything else that's been going on."

"That's my girl. But speaking of that, how was your dad doing today?"

Suddenly her mood changes. "The same. He's just doing poorly. Plus, the rascal sneaks those cigars when we're not looking. We know he's trying hard not to show it, but he's obsessed about the ranch."

Jim is serious. "But I told you to tell him I'd take care of that problem, Ellen. I'm going to talk to him myself. I need for him to trust me." Ellen sits very quietly, not looking at Jim. He glances at her. "You, too. I promise you, you're not going to lose the ranch."

Now she turns to him and speaks rapidly, venting a flood of pent up emotions. "Oh, Jim, you're such a fool! Have you thought of a better plan than that ridiculous train chase?"

He holds the reigns and drives on, not answering her.

"See . . . that's what I thought. And I know you won't give up the idea of going after Arizona Adams and that horrible gang of killers, so you can take over the line. But what you don't understand is that it's *you* that dad's worried about now. The three of us decided we'd much rather lose the ranch than have you—my most precious love and best friend—lose your life!"

Jim looks at her with love and deep compassion. "Please, you and your folks don't need to worry about losing me. But if you lose the ranch . . . well, we've already discussed what that could cause."

Ellen is so dejected by both possibilities that she doesn't bother to answer. Silently they drive on and arrive at the ranch. Jim jumps off and helps Ellen down. The last thing he wants is to argue with her. He puts his arm around her and tries to kiss her, but Ellen struggles out of his embrace. "No, Jim."

"Why not, my darlin' *fiancée*?"

Ellen looks up at him with both love and pain in her eyes. "I'm not your *fiancée* any more, Jim. I'm breaking our engagement."

"Oh come on, you can't be serious, Ellen."

"I am very serious, Jim. As long as you insist on committing suicide by going after Arizona Adams, I can't marry you. I want to be your bride, not your widow!"

Controlling his urge to blurt out the fantastic truth that he's been living with, he says, "But honey, I don't get your reasoning, and besides . . . there are other factors, which I just can't get into with you now. I'm asking you to, please, just let me handle . . ."

Cutting in, she stops him cold. "Good night, Jim." She turns and goes into the house, with tears rolling down her cheeks.

Dumbfounded, Jim stares after her, wondering if he should finally tell Ellen, Helen, and Glen the truth. But he quickly remembers that his reasons for not telling them are as many as the big stars twinkling above. Knowing that he must face this dilemma alone, and never implicate them—or anyone else—in his double-life as the outlaw Arizona Adams, he climbs onto the buckboard and heads back into town.

Chapter 23

The next afternoon Ellen is at her desk in the *Gazette* office, intently working on a story. Jim is turning the dials on the office safe, opens it, and takes out money. He closes the safe and looks at her for a moment. She ignores him. Then to get her attention he says loudly, "Almost forgot, I never got to the bank last Friday. Would you kindly mind the store while I go over to make a deposit?" She continues to work. Trying again, while packing a roll of bills into a leather pouch, he asks anxiously, "Ellen, honey, we're still engaged, aren't we?"

Ellen keeps her eyes down. "Only if you've changed your mind about Arizona Adams."

Jim looks at her working for a moment. "I have to get there before it closes."

As soon as he walks out of the office, she gets up, runs to the *Gazette's* front window and watches him mount his horse with tears in her eyes.

Deeply affected and still not believing that his determination to protect Ellen has caused her to break off their engagement, Jim rides through town ignoring Matt and Myra Tracey and the Coreys—whom he certainly should have thanked again for the hoedown—as they tip their hats to him. He dismounts in front of the bank and passes Hound Dog Bassett, as he enters the bank.

Inside, he walks up to the teller, unaware that Bassett has seized the opportunity to follow him and wait in line just behind him, all the while eavesdropping on his conversation with the teller.

"Pretty hefty deposit ya got there, Mr. Courtney. You holding up banks again?"

Still upset, he snaps, "Wouldn't tell you if I was, would I?"

Bassett's eyes light up. He is listening very intently now.

"Sooner or later you're gonna trip up, y'know." The teller smiles.

Seeing the smile, Jim changes over to their usual joking and banter. "Shh, not so loud, John, we have our standing deal!"

"Don't know about that. We need to renegotiate. What if I were to tip off the sheriff?"

"Well, I'd just take my loot and high-tail it to New York. I got connections there, y'know. The sheriff'll never catch me."

"Maybe yes, maybe no. Better watch it." The teller hands Jim a receipt.

With that, Bassett gets out of line and leaves the bank. Once he's out on Main Street he takes out his notebook and makes some hasty notes. Then he walks across the street to the telegraph office, enters, and gets in line. Following him in is a thin, very prudish-looking older woman, who gets in line behind him. She is the town gossip, Mrs. Willow. The telegraph operator, Mr. Russell, is taking down a telegram coming in over the wires. Bassett finishes writing his telegram and hands it to Mr. Russell, who slowly reads it back to Bassett.

"'To Nicky Shade, 10-25 Gramercy Park, New York, New York: Made heavy deposit today, Whistle Stop Bank. Stop. Learned subject may be planning double-cross and get-away. Stop. Will make this Friday target day. Stop. Signed—Bassett.' Is that what you want?"

"Yes, thank you." Bassett pays for the telegram and leaves. But Mrs. Willow has overheard.

"That's very strange, Mr. Russell. That business about making this Friday the target at the bank."

"Yeah, kinda. That feller's a stranger in town. Cain't tell what he's up to."

"Cain't tell? Why it's as plain as the nose on your face! That man has a very crooked look about him. Sendin' a message to some New York gangster, Nicky, 'bout the heavy deposits on Friday. Sheriff Lynch has to be warned!" She hurries excitedly out of the telegraph office with her misinformation and heads towards the jailhouse.

A few minutes later, Sheriff Lynch is at his desk facing Mrs. Willow. "You sure he said them exact words?"

"Positively! Him and some New York gangster named Nicky are going to rob the bank. Mark my words, sheriff!"

Sheriff Lynch stands up, places his hand on his gun, and says, "Follow me, Mrs. Willow."

The sheriff and Mrs. Willow exit and walk quickly down Main Street to the Assay Hotel. As Mrs. Willow imparts her information to all the townspeople they pass, a curious crowd builds up and follows right after them, chatting excitedly. By the time they arrive in front of the Assay Hotel, they are in a frenzy and ready for action.

The sheriff cups his hands around his mouth and calls out loudly, "Basket, you hear me, Basket? Come out with your hands up. You got till I count to ten. One, two . . ."

Bassett sticks his head out of his window on the second floor, startled by the crowd. "What's the matter? What's going on?"

The sheriff summons his full authority. "What's goin' on, Basket, is you're gittin' outta this town. We know all about you and them New York gangsters. Come down now with all of yer stuff. The next train out is in fifteen minutes and yer gonna be on it! You start any shootin' and you'll find yerself at yer own necktie party! Now move!"

The crowd waits excitedly. Mrs. Willow looks very proud of herself. Sheriff Lynch goes down in a crouch, with his gun pointed at the hotel doorway as Bassett—completely confused, but scared by the town mob—appears with his suitcase and throws his hands up in the air. The crowd rushes forward and grabs him. They start pushing and running him toward the train station.

When they get there with Bassett, his clothes have almost been torn off and he is clutching his suitcase, which has opened up. His clothing is trailing on the ground behind him, along with two boxes of rubber bands. The eastbound train pulls in and the crowd throws Bassett and his suitcase up the stairs into the car. The train starts off, and when it gets a safe distance away, Bassett starts screaming and waving his fist at the cheering crowd on the station platform.

The sheriff is mighty proud standing next to his cohort, Mrs. Willow. "That'll teach them varmints they best not be comin' to Whistle Stop."

Chapter 24

That evening in the Assay Hotel lobby, some of the Directors are talking among themselves while Jim and Beamish, sitting in two old arm chairs, discuss the details of the failed gold shipment plan. Jim says, "I'm afraid we'll have to come up with some other way to deal with Arizona Adams and his gang."

Beamish is secretly concerned about the way Bassett was thrown out of town, and has been trying to work out a new plan to insure that Courtney does not fulfill Joe Curtain's proviso. For now, he plays it tough with Jim, and says, "Obviously. But how? Your gold shipment idea almost got us all killed. Maybe you'd better forget about taking over the Curtain Lines and . . ."

Suddenly shots ring out in the street in front of the hotel. Beamish ducks for cover. Some other Directors hide behind the clerk's counter. Jim goes to a window and looks out, as they hear more shots and wild whooping coming from the street. He shouts, "It's the Adams Gang. Looks like we're in for a wild night!"

The hotel door slams open and two very drunk outlaws brandishing their guns come rolling in looking for the saloon. They fire shots into the ceiling, whooping wildly. Jim immediately recognizes Purdy and Diz and, fearing they will see and recognize him, pulls his hat down, trying to hide his identity. But Purdy does a double-take and calls out, "Hey, ain't you . . ."

Jim turns and starts to walk slowly away, pulling his hat down even further, as the outlaws walk drunkenly in his direction. Suddenly Jim ducks out the side door. The outlaws follow.

Jim runs down the alleyway. Purdy and Diz run drunkenly after him, shouting, "Hey boss, you gotta stop." Jim runs all the way around the building, with them in pursuit. Back in front of the hotel, Jim runs into the lobby again. The Directors and Beamish watch with fear and puzzlement, as Jim dashes past them up the stairs and, at the landing, flings himself into the room on the right.

Jim finds that the room is occupied by a half-dressed, old woman and pushes the door shut behind him. She screams and faints as Jim ducks into her closet full of dresses, and quickly closes that door behind him.

The two gang members run into the lobby, look around, and dash up the stairs. Not seeing Jim in the hall, Diz says, "He done disappeared, Purdy. He sure don't wanna see us, and he knows best. We gotta split this town, afore he gets angry at us."

Disappointed, Purdy complains, "Damn! No dingle dippin' fer us tonight! I wuz right needy." With that, Diz laughs and gives Purdy a shove. They run back down the stairs and rush out of the Assay lobby into the night. The dumbfounded Directors and Beamish then rush up the stairs and crash into the old woman's room. She has regained consciousness, and fearfully points to her closet. Beamish opens the closet door, and he and the Directors find Jim crouching among the dresses.

Jim whispers, "Are they gone?"

Beamish is totally contemptuous. "Yes. You can come out now. You're safe. They won't hurt you."

The other Directors are crowded in the doorway, and are now convinced that Jim is a bigger coward than any of them. They talk among themselves as if he is not there.

Beamish exclaims to Felix Herkimer, "Hiding behind a woman's skirt!"

Herkimer looks down at Jim. "Down on his knees in a closet!"

Dilbert Findley says, "The guy's a dyed-in-the-wool coward!"

Will Toomey agrees. "He's a yellow-belly. Yellow as they come!"

Jim says nothing in his defense as Beamish and the Directors—unified in their agreement about his cowardice—file out of the room.

*

The next morning in the town square Beamish stops to talk with some townspeople. "Never seen anything like it! Jim Courtney isn't a bad sort, but the man lacks spine, I'm afraid." Beamish continues to spread the word of Jim's "cowardice" all over town—to loiterers in front of the dance hall, to townspeople on the hotel porch, and to folks at the general store, telegraph office, train station, and blacksmith's shop.

*

Later that morning Ellen, wearing a flowered dress and bonnet, is walking down Main Street on her way to the general store. As she walks along, with her head held high, people stare at her, then quickly cast their eyes down as she passes. All but Tommy and his pal Mike, that is, who are coming toward her having a great old time pretending to be Arizona Adams and Jim. Mike has a toy gun with which he menaces Tommy, who—as soon as Ellen gets close enough—takes the part of Jim and gets down on his knees and prays. "Please, please, Mr. Adams, don't kill me, don't kill me." Deeply annoyed, Ellen passes the two pranksters, as some town vagrants sitting on the fence in front of the feed store watch.

One vagrant winks to the others, as he decides to join in on the taunting of Ellen. He chuckles and says, "Watch this!"

He gets down from the fence and walks behind Ellen, pretending to look behind her skirt. As they walk on, Ellen becomes aware that he is following her. She turns and faces the smirking vagrant. "Why are you following me?"

"Beggin' yer pardon, ma'am, I warn't followin' yuh."

"Then what are you doing?"

"Well, ma'am, I was just lookin' to see if Jim Courtney was hidin' behind your skirt."

Ellen stares at the vagrant for a moment. Then she smiles sweetly at him. "You have a fine sense of humor. Let me show you something." She walks up to the vagrant.

He's smiling broadly for the benefit of his pals. "Whadda yuh gonna show me?"

Ellen smiles too. "This!" She swings her leg back, then swings it forward and kicks him hard on the shin. "I just wanted to show you how hard I can kick."

The vagrant doubles over, hopping around in pain. His friends and the two boys break out in laughter.

She is not amused. "Did I hurt you? I'm so sorry. If Jim were behind me, that kick would have hit him too—so I guess he's not behind my skirt. Seems to me *you* are." She kicks him in his other shin, doubling his pain and the tempo of his hopping and screaming. "Bye. Have a lovely day." Ellen proceeds to the general store.

As Ellen buys her groceries, other patrons look in her direction and talk among themselves. She thinks, "I just can't believe this is happening." Tears suddenly roll down her cheeks. Standing in the back of the store where no one can see, she takes out her handkerchief and dabs her eyes. "Jim, oh Jim! What on earth has happened to you?"

Chapter 25

That same morning, Grady confronts Purdy and Diz in the hideout cabin. "Now that you two drunkards have slept it off, you best tell me exactly what you saw in town last night."

Purdy is nervous. "Yeah, we wuz drunk and mebbe dumb to go to town, but I swear, Grady, the guy at that hotel looked just like Arizona."

Diz pipes in, "He was lovey-dovey with them thar big shots fer sure."

Grady is puzzled. "Don't make no sense. You guys ain't spooked now are you?"

Purdy gets huffy. "No way, Grady, we're cold sober an' in our right minds."

Grady looks at them for a minute, then he gets an idea. "Wait a minute, now, mebbe it does make some sense! Somebody seems to know all the moves we make. Who would know that better'n Arizona! What the devil . . . I do believe it *is* him! He musta struck some kinda deal with them rail line biggy wigs to do us in! That's why he ain't showed up here fer so long. The traitor!"

Diz is indignant now. "Why don't we go back to Whistle Stop and bust him up, in fact kill him?"

Grady's thoughtful. "I got a better idea, much better."

Purdy leans forward, all ears. "What?"

Grady pushes him back, not wanting Purdy's stench in his face. "The guy you boys seen *wasn't* Arizona Adams."

Diz defends himself, knowing he isn't a liar. "Oh, come on, Grady! We warn't that blind drunk!"

Grady says, dead sure, "You maybe wasn't. But that guy could'na been Arizona."

Now Purdy is defiant. "Why the Jeezus not?"

Grady replies, proud as can be, "Because, boys, *I* am Arizona Adams!"

Purdy is amazed. "Are you plumb loco?"

Diz challenges him. "What have *you* been drinkin'?"

Grady, brimming with bravado, spells out his view of what's happened. "Yeah, I'm loco—like a fox! Think about it. If he's made a deal with them dudes, then Arizona ain't never gonna come back here. But nobody else knows that 'cept us. Meanwhile, everyone 'round here is scared to death of him. So, if these yokels was tuh get an idea that somethin' had happened to Arizona, they'd mebbe start feelin' brave enough to really start fightin' back. So we gotta not let 'em know it ain't Arizona leadin' us no more. That means Arizona and his men is gonna keep right on doin' what they been doin', robbin' the Curtain Rail Lines trains. And, since nobody in this territory ain't ever seen Arizona without his mask on, you are now looking at none other than Arizona Adams hisself— me! Get it, boys?"

Purdy and Diz stare at Grady, look at each other, then back at Grady. Starting to get his logic, Purdy says, "Well ain't that the darndest thing I ever heard."

Diz gets it too. "Golly, gee . . . boss."

Satisfied with himself, Grady reaches for the bottle and glasses on the table and pours a round of drinks. They all raise their glasses and Grady toasts himself, "To the *new* Arizona Adams! And we'll be usin' *my* rules from now on."

*

The next morning, out on the flatlands, Grady, dressed in black as Arizona Adams, and the gang are in a full gallop, bearing down on a train. With guns blasting away at the engine cab, they force the train to stop. The masked outlaws board the passenger cars. In one car the conductor attempts to hold the door closed, but Grady shoots him right through the door window. He collapses in pain. Grady and the gang enter the car. The passengers cower. Grady yells out, "Did y'all get that, everyone? If you don't wanna be next ya kin take out your valuables and give them to my men as they pass by." Corky, Gyp and several other gang members pass through the aisle collecting the loot, while Grady heads for the baggage car with Diz and Purdy.

Grady and the men enter the baggage car. The guard goes to pull his gun. Grady shoots him. "Alright men, blow that safe." They dynamite the safe and pack their saddle bags with the payroll money they find inside.

Grady and the gang take off across the prairie.

Chapter 26

Later that same morning, Beamish and the Directors are meeting around a long table in the back room of the Assay Hotel Saloon. Beamish addresses the Directors. "As former second in command, I am now forced to take full charge. It's very obvious that we must have new and dependable leadership to hunt for Arizona Adams and his gang. We have all demonstrated our courage, that's true, but realistically speaking, men, we are going to have a hard time trying to defeat these cutthroats at their own game in their home territory. We need a new plan, and quickly! So let's put our thinking caps on. We can't out-shoot them, but we *can* out-think them!

The Directors are paying close attention to Beamish, as Jim comes in and stands quietly at the back of the room. Beamish sees him and—no longer concerned about him—completely ignores him and continues, "We all know that if the Curtain Rail Lines is to survive, we must expand our territory. If we were to be successful in our attempts to defeat these outlaws, our next move would be to put pressure on certain senators in Washington—that we know to be friends—for a new land grant out here in the Arizona Territory. In addition, to get back in the black, we will foreclose on every ranch or farm that falls one mortgage payment behind, and take back their ranches. We appropriated lands and properties when Joe Curtain was running the company, and we can do it again. Using these methods, we will expand westward at a rock-bottom level of expense, and surely show a profit.

Will Toomey, who used to live among ranchers in Montana, questions Beamish. "Wait a minute, Albert, a lot of folks around here will lose their ranches and farms with that plan. Ranching and farming are cyclical . . . you have good years and bad. Doesn't mean they're not loyal customers that will nurture the land and continue to pay us interest for years to come."

Beamish, sensing that Toomey may not like his tactics, replies defiantly, "Too bad if they can't afford to pay their mortgage. They're standing in the way of progress. Business is business. Like I said, we did it before, and we can do it again."

Will Toomey looks away, none too happy.

Jim is outwardly calm listening to the greedy plan spewing from Beamish's mouth, but inwardly his blood is boiling with each utterance. He wants to strangle Beamish, but restrains himself.

Determined, Beamish looks around to see if there are any other protestors. No other Director speaks up. Satisfied, he hammers home his meaning. "The day is not far off when we can expect a vote by the stockholders. Unless we can show them a real increase in business, out of the red, toward substantial expansion and profits, we'll each be in deep trouble that will deprive us of our livelihoods." Now he takes a smug glance at Jim. "We must keep the leadership of the Curtain Lines in seasoned, capable hands."

Some of the Directors call out, "Whose hands?"

Beamish stands tall. "Ours, with me as chairman!"

Just then the telegraph messenger, Tom, knocks on the door and enters. "We just got a wire from up the line that the Adams Gang attacked the morning train. They shot a conductor and a guard and made off with the payroll." He tips his hat and shuts the door.

There's dead silence for a moment, followed by a general commotion.

"We're bankrupt for sure."

"That damn gang is gonna take us down."

"How in the world can we ever stop them?"

Jim is bursting out of his skin, knowing that Grady is now completely out of control, and so is Beamish.

Beamish raises his arms and yells out, "Quiet men. Quiet down. Yes, that's the last straw, but listen up. I have a plan."

A hush grows among them, as they all turn to look at Beamish. Will Toomey says, "We're listening, Al, this better be damn good."

Beamish looks around. "All right, here's my plan. I say we employ the kind of tactics we excel at—business tactics! With the help of . . . " he looks at Jim and then uses a condescending voice, "our former unfortunate leader, Mr. Jim Courtney, we will run a front page story in the *Whistle Stop Gazette* offering twenty-thousand shares of preferred stock in the Curtain Rail Lines, par value five dollars per share, to Arizona Adams and his men, to be issued at the rate of four-thousand shares per year for the next five years, if Arizona Adams will present himself to us and sign a contract guaranteeing not to attack any of our trains ever again. If the bargain is not kept, the shares will either not be disbursed or the agreement will be revoked and rendered null and void. It will further say that Adams and his gang must meet with us in the back room of this hotel next Monday morning at 10 A.M. Well, gentlemen, that's my plan. I think it's the only way. How say you? All in favor raise your hands."

The Directors' hands shoot up unanimously. Beamish is gratified. "It is so agreed. I see Mr. Courtney back there. Will you cooperate, sir?" All eyes turn to look at Jim.

Jim—seeing that Beamish's plan provides him with an opportunity—looks Beamish in the eye, and says, "Yes."

Beamish smiles triumphantly. "Then we would appreciate it, sir, if you would quickly arrange to issue a special edition of your paper featuring our business offer. And, of course, we extend our sympathies to you for your inability to carry out the conditions which would have allowed you to lay claim to the Curtain Rail Lines. Too bad, Mr. Courtney."

Jim looks at Beamish with masked contempt and leaves, now knowing exactly what he must do.

Chapter 27

At the *Gazette* office the next morning, Jim and Ellen, still estranged, silently watch through the window as the townspeople react to the story of the Curtain Rail Lines executives' offer to the Adams Gang. After a few minutes, facing forward, Jim comments, "It's got them talking. The gang will surely get wind of it."

Not looking at him either, she retorts, "Yes, but Arizona Adams may smell a trap."

Jim does not react to the mention of Arizona. "Yup. He could. But we won't know until Monday morning at 10 A.M., when the meeting is scheduled to take place. Much as I hate to say it, I must give Beamish credit for the idea."

Forlorn, she says, "Just a few days from now." Then dropping her guard, she turns and speaks her mind. "Oh Jim, I am praying with all my heart that it works. Because I know you're still planning on getting Arizona, and, like I've said too many times, I just know that you're no match for such a cold, calculating outlaw. The odds would be stacked against you in a shootout with him."

Jim understands her deepening fear, because of Grady's latest shooting spree. He acts bitter about being labeled a coward. "Yeah, sure, the whole town thinks that by now, don't they?"

"Let them think what they like. I don't care."

"Yeah, but they think I'm alive only because I'm good at hiding behind a woman's skirt. How can I live with that?"

Now she looks up into his eyes with love. "I don't believe that for one second, Jim Courtney. It's hogwash. I know you had your reasons for ducking those outlaws. The only thing is, I sure don't know what your reasons were." Ellen throws her arms around Jim and embraces him.

He is so glad to hold her in his arms that he's again tempted to reveal his secret. "Well, I'll tell you, Ellen, and you may find this real hard to believe, my reason was . . ." But as she looks up at him expectantly, her innocent and trusting face makes him decide to tell her exactly what he thought when the outlaws showed up. "My reason was that Arizona Adams wasn't with those men. That's it. There was no point in tangling with two drunk outlaws that just didn't matter. Of course, I didn't figure on Beamish spreading the word that I was a coward. So, please, let's just forget it. We've got another edition to lock up. Let's get to it."

Ellen—glad for his explanation but still confused about why they were chasing him to begin with—is unwilling to press him further. "Thanks for letting me know, Jim, but I still don't want you going after Arizona, and don't you forget that."

"How could I?"

She cracks a smile, picks up her pencil, and Jim starts dictating notes for a news story.

*

Later that same afternoon, back at the gang's hideout, Grady is reading the front page of the *Gazette*, with Purdy, Gyp, Diz, Corky and some of the other gang members waiting to hear what it says. Grady is amazed. "Well, ain't that a fine how do ya do. Those Curtain dudes are offerin' us a deal! Twenty thousand shares of stock in the Curtain Rail Lines at five dollars a share if we'll lay off robbin' their trains!"

Purdy, who is sitting next to Grady, rubs his hands together, smelling big money. He says, "Geez, Grady, let's grab it. And then we'll just keep right on robbin' the trains."

Gyp smells big money too. "Yeah, Grady, take the deal!" The other men nod. All seem to like the deal.

Grady swiftly punches Purdy's arm. "Now you see why I'm the leader of this bunch of lunkheads. Didn't it ever occur to ya that maybe this is a trap?"

Purdy shows some respect as he rubs his arm where Grady hit him. "Jeez, do ya think it is, boss?"

Grady gets up and ponders for a minute, pacing back and forth. Then he stops. "No, gol' darn it, on second thought ah don't believe it's no trap. See now, they know they cain't stop us in a gunfight. So they figger to stop us another way, with this here plan. Besides, who's gonna trap us? Sheriff Lynch? C'mon, he ain't got no army and he's gonna be hidin' in his outhouse if we ride into town. Everyone know'd that, so them Curtain fancy pants musta fixed this deal with him. And as for Arizona, the last thing he wants is tuh be exposed as Arizona Adams, 'specially since them people got shot up in the last few train attacks. Arizona's smart enough tuh know that if we ride into town one of us is gonna be posin' as Arizona Adams, or else we wouldn't be ridin' in tuh make the deal. So, in the meetin' we don't recognize him and yuh kin bet every dollar yuh got he won't be showin' no signs of knowin' us neither. No, siree, Arizona ain't dumb. Only one smarter'n him is me, the new Arizona Adams. Get it?"

Gyp is on board. "Gol' darn, then we take up their offer, Grady? I mean, Arizona."

Grady Profit is full of himself. "Get ready to get rich this comin' Monday mornin'!"

Chapter 28

The long hand on the wall clock moves from ten to nine minutes of ten.

A group of townspeople have gathered in the lobby of the Assay Hotel. One man speaks nervously. "Nine more minutes. Well, I gotta go and close up my shop. I ain't takin' no chances. Last time they was in town, they shot up all the new shoes I just got shipped in from New York and busted my windows, to boot."

They all hurry out of the lobby onto Main Street, where some other townspeople are busy boarding up their shop windows while others run to seek safety in bars and shops.

Back in the hotel lobby, the clock's minute hand moves to seven minutes to the hour. Luke, the room clerk, takes a big sip of whiskey.

In all of the store fronts, sets of eyes peer out. Scattered around town, frightened faces intently look up the street, waiting for the Adams Gang.

The Assay Hotel clock shows exactly 10 A.M., as the church bell rings the hour.

On Main Street, since there is no sign of the Adams Gang, townspeople cautiously begin to emerge from their hiding places and discuss the situation.

A merchant says, "They ain't comin', the yellah bellies!"

The blacksmith mocks the others. "Didja see how all them people was hidin', scared outta their underwear?"

The vagrant who taunted Ellen jibes at the blacksmith, "I kinda think *your* underwear may need launderin' too, mister blacksmith!" He laughs out loud.

They all start to walk tall again, when suddenly they hear pounding hooves. They turn as a band of horsemen appears at the top of the hill, where Main Street leads into Whistle Stop.

The merchant yells frantically, "It's them! They're comin'!"

The brave-talking townspeople quickly rush back into their hiding places, and watch the gang as they thunder into town.

*

Grady, unmasked and dressed in Arizona Adams' black outfit, leads the way, followed by the rest of the gang. They gallop up to the entrance of the Assay Hotel where they dismount. Grady talks in a low voice. "Now remember, boys, once we're in there, don't show you recognize Arizona. It'll give the whole game away if you do." They all nod in agreement and go into the lobby of the hotel.

Inside, Luke gulps another shot as they enter, and says, "Right, right, right this way, gents." They all follow the quaking clerk through the door to the empty saloon and on to the back room.

Luke, scared to death, steps out of the way as the outlaws file past him into the back room and stand together near the door, their hands resting on their guns. Beamish and the Directors are waiting, standing along the right side of the long table. A few tension-filled seconds pass. There's a silent face-off.

Then Beamish steps forward, hesitantly. "Good morning, gentlemen, very nice of you to be so prompt. I am Mr. Beamish, chairman of the board of directors of the Curtain Rail Lines, and these are the other Directors, uh, my partners . . . uh, pardners. May I ask which of you is Arizona Adams?"

Grady steps forward. "Me!"

Beamish looks into his eyes. "Well, well, so we meet at last. This is a real pleasure, mister, uh, Arizona Adams." He offers a falsely cordial handshake, which Grady ignores.

Beamish pulls back his hand. "Well now, please take the empty seats on that side of the table, gents, and we will proceed with the business at hand. My Directors will each take a seat on the other side of the table, ah, exactly where they are now."

They all take their seats as indicated. Beamish is happy that went well. "Very good. I will now call the meeting to order."

Grady is defiant. "We ain't orderin' nuthin'. This ain't no time fer drinkin'. Git on with the business."

Beamish is officious. "Oh, yes, but we have to conduct the business according to usual business formalities. Mr. Henry Travis over there is our secretary, and he will be recording the minutes of the meeting."

Grady is annoyed. "Don't he know the time? It's about ten minutes after ten. What's so important about the minutes?"

Beamish now comprehends Arizona's total lack of understanding about business, and worries that he really does not know what the deal means. "Just a formality, Mr. Arizona. Now, since you are all here, I assume that you are familiar with the terms of our offer, uh, from a business perspective."

Grady is still annoyed. "Yeah, but 'cept fer me and Purdy here nobody else kin read, so I got familiar with yer offer and told it ta the boys." The door to the room opens and Jim enters. All heads turn in his direction. The outlaws glance at one another, but not one of them registers the slightest sign of recognition.

Likewise, Jim looks at all of them, and says nothing.

Beamish introduces him. "Gentlemen, this is Mr. James Courtney, the publisher and editor of your very fine local newspaper, the *Whistle Stop Gazette*."

Grady is astounded. "What?"

Purdy's face shows amazement. "He writes the paper?"

Gyp exclaims incredulously, "He's a editor and publishes it?"

Ben mumbles, "Ah jes don't believe it!"

Diz says, "How could that be?"

Beamish is amazed at their reaction. "Oh, yes, I guess it is surprising. He does seem rather young to hold such an important position in this town. Just recently, he, uh, had reason to become interested in the Curtain Lines, so we asked him to be here."

Grady is in shock. "If that don't beat all!" But he watches Arizona—or James Courtney—like a hawk, as he takes a seat at the end of the table. He sees Arizona stare right back at him, but he's poker-faced. Just as Grady predicted, the real Arizona Adams is not showing one speck of recognition for the gang.

Beamish pushes a stack of papers toward Grady. "We will now pass the contracts around for your inspection, gentlemen. You'll see I've already signed them. Just take two copies each and pass the rest on to the gentleman seated next to you." The outlaws each take their copies and pass the rest on from man to man.

The Directors, all at the same time, take expensive pens from inside their suit coat pockets, and, as in a rhythm ballet, place them on the table in front of them, with the points facing the outlaw seated opposite each of them.

In response the outlaws, all at the same time, draw their guns from their holsters and place them on the table in front of them, with the barrels pointing directly at the Director in front of each of them. Then the outlaws all reach for the pens in unison, and the Directors cringe back in their chairs.

The outlaws glance at the contract, then look at each other helplessly, since they can't read. Then they all look at Grady, who is busy reading it. After a minute or so, Grady looks up. "Seems okay to me . . . says we're the party of the first part."

Beamish foolishly thinks everything is going well. "Alright, gentlemen, if you have finished studying the contract, are there any questions?"

Gyp is puzzled. "Yeah. What does it say?"

At this point Jim gets up to leave the room, kind of shaking his head in disbelief. Beamish is now nervous. "Well, it's essentially what the newspaper story said."

Grady watches Arizona depart, then explains to the gang, "Listen boys, it is just like I told ya. It says we stop robbin' the trains, and they give us twenty thousand shares of stock in the rail line, worth five bucks a share." He looks at Beamish. "Right?"

Beamish is relieved. "Absolutely! Are you agreed on this matter?"

Looking down at the contract again, Grady reads, "To be issued to us over the next five years. Four thousand shares every year."

Beamish wants to close. "Agreed?"

Grady looks up. "Yup."

Beamish breaks into a big smile. "I must say, you men are certainly shrewd businessmen! Absolutely are! So now are you ready to sign the contract? If you are, just sign your name where you see the blank line at the bottom of each copy, keep one for yourself, pass the other to me, and we're in business."

One of the outlaws speaks. "My name is Ben. I know it begins with a capital B but I dunno how to do the rest of it."

Beamish accommodates him. "Oh, I see. Well, you can put a B. And if any of you don't know how to write your name, or at least the first letter, just make an X."

As the contracts are signed and passed back to Beamish, he looks at one after another. Ben's has a B. Grady's and Purdy's have their signatures. All the rest are signed with an X. "Excellent work, gentlemen. May I now congratulate you on your good fortune! And since you are now shareholders in the Curtain Rail Lines, we can all look forward to unparalleled prosperity and good will, since you will never again apply your talents to robbing our trains. In honor of this historic occasion, I propose that we all adjourn to the saloon and toast our promising future together."

The Directors pick up their pens and the outlaws pick up their guns and contracts, and they all depart to the saloon.

Jim is already there having a drink, looking real tough, as he watches the outlaws and Directors come in and line up further down the bar. They're all happily congratulating one another on their mutually beneficial deal. Two customers who were at the bar quickly leave.

Grady whispers to Purdy, "Sure enough! It *is* that rat fink, Arizona! Wha' did I tell ya? He's got an *interest* in the rail line."

Purdy continues the conversation in a whisper. "You sure had him pegged, but what'll happen to our deal if they find out you ain't Arizona and *he* is?"

Surprised by the sense of Purdy's question, he quickly says, "We can kiss the deal goodbye! The whole damn shootin' match will be *finito*."

Purdy glances down the bar at Arizona. "We gotta do somethin', Grady, and quick! 'Cause he looks pretty pissed to me."

Beamish walks up to the two outlaws with three glasses of whiskey in his hand. He offers one to each of them. "Well, Mr. Arizona, and Mr. . . . ?"

"Purdy."

"We're pardners now, right?" He raises his glass.

Grady holds his glass up with one hand. "Sure thing," he says, and puts his other arm hard around Beamish's shoulder. "When do we get the first payment, pardner?"

Beamish, disliking the weight of his arm, tries to take charge. "The second we get back to New York I will instruct the book-keeping department to immediately disburse four thousand shares as our first payment, to show you our good faith. You all signed the contract, so it's a legal, closed deal. We can send the shares here, to the Whistle Stop telegraph office. How's that, Arizona?"

Slipping his arm off of Beamish's shoulder, Grady puts his glass on the bar and fingers his gun suggestively. "Good. Then there'll be no problems, eh?"

Just then, Beamish gets an idea. "Well, none from us Directors."

Grady is suspicious. "None from you. But maybe from someone else?"

Beamish looks down the bar at Jim, then lowers his voice and speaks conspiratorially. "Well, I suppose I should warn you, out of a feeling for a fellow pardner, of course, that Jim Courtney, the editor fellah, might be inclined to write some unfavorable things about this deal in the *Whistle Stop Gazette*. For some reason he doesn't seem to like you. Of course, if he was to find a legal loophole, he sure could write about it, and it *could* come to the attention of the Arizona Territorial Legislature."

Grady is suddenly perturbed. "That *is* a problem." He stares at Jim, who's drinking further down the bar.

Grady says to Beamish, "'Scuse me." Grady walks down to Jim and elbows a director aside. Grady says to Willie, the bartender, "Two Sidewinders. One for my friend there." He indicates Jim. Willie mixes the drinks and pours the Sidewinders in front of Grady and Jim.

Jim raises his glass in a salute to Grady. Sardonically he says, "To your good fortune, Mr. Arizona Adams."

Grady uses a mean voice. "I hear you don't like me."

Jim plays it cool and says, very close to Grady's ear, "Well now, I don't believe I came right out and said that. But, just because you shot and killed some innocent people on the train, and probably killed Sage too, why would that cause me not to like you?"

Grady smirks, and says, "Smart apple, huh? Nobody seen me shoot 'em."

"So the truth of the matter must be that they shot themselves." Now Jim speaks loudly, so the whole room can hear him. "Is that what you want me to think, Arizona Adams?"

Grady takes his loud voice as a challenge, and responds even louder, "You're diggin' your own grave with your tongue! You asked for it! I'm callin' you out, Courtney! If you ain't as yellah as I hear tell everybody knows you are, meet me at six this evenin' on Main Street." To the other outlaws, he says, "C'mon boys, let's git outta here." They all take a gander at Jim as they troop out of the bar.

As Grady passes Beamish, he winks and says, in a very low voice, "That'll take care of the problem, pardner. No shootin' in the back. I'll gun him down in front of everybody in a duel, all legal."

Jim downs his drink as he watches them go.

Chapter 29

Around noon, in the garden at the Williams ranch, Ellen paces before Jim as she expresses her feelings. "You've really done it this time, Jim! I knew it! I knew this had to happen! I begged you to avoid this."

Jim takes Ellen in his arms. "I'm sorry darlin'. It couldn't be avoided, not without the whole town thinking me the biggest coward in the entire Western territory. Please try to understand."

She pushes away from him. "I understand only too well that you've allowed him to set you up to be killed at six this evening, when I want you alive." She looks up at him with true fear in her eyes. "Oh, Jim, I love you and I need you. What good will your foolish honor be when you're dead and gone?"

He sees her agony. "What do you want me to do?"

"There's a train leaving town at four o'clock. Get on it. Go to Santa Fe, Chicago, New York, go anywhere until this nightmare is over. Please, Jim, please!"

He frowns. "I'd do anything for you, Ellen, but this . . ."

She is suddenly adamant. "Jim, unless you show some sense and get out of town, our engagement is finally, definitely over. I mean it this time!"

He tries to reason. "Aw, come on, honey, I have to face him. Don't forget you also stand to lose your ranch, and there's your dad . . ."

She cuts in. "Jim, face it, like I've said too many times, you have no chance! You're a journalist, not a gunslinger."

He smiles. "You need to have faith in me, sweetheart. You never give me credit for the fighting I actually did in the Spanish American War, and that was darn bloody. Meanwhile, I have to get to town and set my affairs in order." Jim kisses Ellen but she remains unresponsive. He mounts his horse and rides toward town. Ellen is positive she will never kiss him again.

*

Back at the outlaws' hideout, Grady sits at the table with Purdy, Gyp, Diz, Corky, and Ben. "After I kill Courtney tonight, we ain't gonna rob the trains no more."

Gyp smiles. "Yeah, we're gonna be sweet little angels."

Grady says, "Angels with smokin' guns!"

Ben is puzzled. "But you just said we ain't gonna . . ."

"Thass right, Ben! I said we ain't gonna rob the trains. But that contract don't say nothin' about robbin' stagecoaches, banks, ranches, and farms, does it?"

The light bulb goes on in Ben's weak mind. "Thass right! Grady, yer plumb smarter'n a snake's grandfather!"

Acting the kingpin, Grady says, "All right. Now we don't want no slip-ups tonight. Purdy, you and Gyp will be my backups. Purdy, you'll be on the hotel roof, and Gyp will be hiding over near the dance hall. Got it?" Purdy and Gyp nod.

"I'll beat Arizona to the draw. But if anything goes wrong, gun him down quick. We'll all be livin' high on the hog after tonight!"

*

At the Williams ranch, later that afternoon, Helen Williams stands beside her daughter, who sits on the bed next to her father. Ellen is bitter, as she expresses her fears. "Sheriff Lynch is the real coward or he would not allow this to happen. And I'm afraid all of Jim's friends in town are frightened to death of Arizona Adams, because not one of them has had the courage to say they'd help him! And those crooked Directors probably want him dead."

Glen Williams struggles to rise from his bed. "Jim has one friend whose help he can depend on."

Ellen tries to settle him. "You?"

Glen tries to get up again. "You bet! Helen, fetch me my gun."

Helen is worried. "Glen, lie still! You can't help Jim by killing yourself."

"Dad, you can't even walk. All we can do now is pray for a miracle. What time is it? Every minute seems so endless."

Helen Williams puts her hand on her daughter's arm. "It's 5:26. You've got to get hold of yourself too, Ellen. The Lord knows you've tried every possible way to get Jim to stop this foolishness, but he answered by asking you to have faith in him, so that's what you must do. Have faith in him! He fought in the war with Spain, went to Paris for the treaty, and stayed to learn the newspaper business. I'd say he's one of the smartest men I've ever known—and without showing off or acting superior."

Ellen stands up and sobs. "What I know is that Arizona Adams is one of the meanest outlaws to ever come out of the West. I'm heading for town. I hope I'm not too late." She leaves the bedroom, and when she passes through the living room she pauses. Then she gets her dad's rifle, takes the box of bullets, and loads it. Outside, Ellen mounts her horse, lays the rifle across her saddle, and races off filled with fear.

*

Just a few minutes ahead of her, Grady is already leading the gang members on a fast gallop toward Whistle Stop.

Chapter 30

In the back room at the Assay Saloon, the Directors are gathered. Felix Herkimer makes his predictions. "Courtney is as good as dead. We all know he's a bigger coward than any of us, and probably Arizona Adams heard about it, too. That's why he was surprised when Courtney agreed to this gunfight."

Will Toomey is puzzled. "Well for a smart guy, he's also turned out to be a bigger fool than any of us. And I wonder why Arizona forced this fight on him anyway? A man he just met. All Courtney did was raise his voice to Arizona."

Felix engages Will. "It doesn't matter if they just met face to face, 'cause Arizona sure knew him by name. Didn't you see how they all reacted when he was introduced? Courtney's been reporting on the Adams Gang in the *Gazette* for a long time. The pen can be mightier than the gun. You can bet Arizona thinks Courtney will keep on writing bad things about him and the gang that'll stir up the people and ruin our deal."

Beamish plays it cool, acting the observer. "Well, from my view, Courtney asked for it, starting that fight in the bar."

Henry adds, "No matter now. What time is it?"

Felix looks at his pocket watch. "Ten minutes to six." Just then, Jim enters the room. He has strapped on two holsters, each holding a Colt 45.

Beamish, secretly looking forward to seeing Jim get gunned down, acts magnanimous. "See, boys, Jim's not the coward some of you thought he was. Look at him. Here he is, all ready to go out like a man! Didn't run at all like you thought he would. Maybe that's not too smart, but we must give him credit, right boys?" They all nod. Beamish looks at Jim. "Good luck, pardner, and we're all real sorry it had to end this way."

Jim takes in the room full of varmints, and acts humble. "Yeah, sure. Thanks a lot."

Beamish checks his watch. "Just five minutes to go. You better get out on the street." He laughs. "Maybe Arizona will get cold feet and not show up."

Jim gives Beamish a cold stare.

Beamish stares back with snake eyes.

Then they all file out of the saloon.

Jim and the Directors walk out onto Main Street. The street is completely empty. The sheriff and the mayor are nowhere to be seen. All the townsfolk are behind doors and peeking out of windows. Suddenly hearing thundering hooves, they all look up the street, where in the distance they see Arizona Adams and his gang riding toward the hotel.

Beamish says to the Directors, "We better take cover." Beamish offers his hand to Jim. "Nice knowing you, Courtney."

Jim shakes Beamish's hand and says, sarcastically, "I sure appreciate your honesty, Beamish."

All the Directors quickly duck into the lobby of the hotel.

The gang rides up, dismounts, and except for Grady, they all file into the hotel lobby too. Jim sees that Purdy and Gyp are missing.

Then Jim and Grady are alone on the street, facing one another.

In the hotel lobby, Beamish, the other Directors, and the gang members glance up at the clock on the wall. The clock shows one minute to six.

Back on Main Street, Grady and Jim slowly walk toward one another.

In the hotel lobby, the minute hand jumps to exactly six o'clock.

The church bell rings the hour.

On Main Street, both men swiftly draw their guns and fire. Jim staggers and falls. Grady falls, too.

Then Purdy, standing on the roof of the hotel, fires at Jim and misses. Jim rolls over and quickly fans the trigger of his gun, hitting Purdy, who falls off of the roof to the ground, obviously dead.

Another shot whizzes past Jim, and he rolls again and shoots Gyp, who has stepped from behind a post near the dance hall. Jim sees Gyp fall dead, and then he loses consciousness himself.

The townspeople emerge very cautiously from their hiding places. The remaining gang members run out of the hotel, mount up, and race out of town, past Ellen. She rides into town in a full cantor, scared when she sees that the Directors and townspeople are coming out onto Main Street.

Felix Herkimer is awed. "I never saw anything like it!"

Will Toomey is amazed. "I can't believe it!"

Henry Travis is shocked. "Courtney out-gunned them!"

Ellen dismounts—her father's rifle falling to the ground—and runs to Jim. The gathering crowd makes way for her. He has been shot in the head. Ellen stoops to him, crying, and takes his head in her arms.

Some of the other townspeople, joined by the sheriff and mayor, who have suddenly appeared, are gathering around Grady. They are excited. Virgil, the burley drunk, asks, "Is he dead?"

The sheriff reaches down and feels his pulse. "Deader'n a doornail. I'll be darned, he wuz shot right through the heart!"

Many of the townspeople start to repeat, "Arizona Adams is dead, Arizona Adams is dead!"

Beamish asks no one in particular, "Is Courtney dead?"

Felix looks at Jim on the ground. "He hasn't moved."

Beamish leans in for a closer look, while whispering triumphantly, "He's a goner. The company's mine!"

As Ellen sobs over Jim, his eyes slowly open. Blood is trickling from the wound in his scalp. "What happened?"

Ellen is extremely surprised and utterly happy. "Jim, oh Jim, thank God you're alive!" While kissing and hugging him frantically, she yells to the crowd, "Quick! Somebody get the doc over here."

Jim looks up at Ellen. "Is, uh, Arizona . . . ?"

Felix says excitedly, "Arizona's dead! Never saw such sharpshooting in my life, Courtney! Wasn't that great, Mr. Beamish?"

Beamish is bitter. "Great is hardly the word to describe it."

Chapter 31

There are now two beds in the bedroom at the Williams ranch. Glen Williams is in the double bed and Jim, with his head bandaged, is in the single bed. Glen looks over at his roommate. "You up to a few hands of poker, Mr. Dead Eye Dick?"

Jim props himself up. "Ready, willing, and almost able."

They both climb slowly out of their beds and seat themselves at a small table in the center of the room. Glen deals a hand. "Y'know, Jim, I heard everybody's wonderin' how a small town newspaper editor got to be a world class sharpshooter. I'm wonderin' myself, 'cause when you was a young feller, you could hardly hit a ruptured elephant in the behind."

Jim is sheepish. "Don't know how I did it either. I guess you'd just have to call it beginner's luck, but—just like your daughter— you're forgetting that I learned how to shoot a rifle for the Spanish American War."

Glen looks closely at Jim, and he's got a different thought in mind. "Well, that may be, but you sure developed skills with a Colt 45 just when you needed them."

Jim looks at his cards. "Sure seems so. I guess I'm a natural."

Glen looks up from his cards. "Y'know, Jim, this feller Arizona Adams was a real strange one."

"How so?"

"Well, lyin' here with nothin' to do but count the cracks in the ceilin', I done a little thinkin'."

Jim is cautious. "What came of that?"

Glen looks at him hard. "Well, it come to me that maybe this feller Arizona Adams was really *two* different fellers, not one."

"Don't see how that could be, Glen. How do you figure that?"

Glen scratches his head. "Arizona started off as a gang leader, but under it all, he was a real good bad guy, so to speak. He raided the trains, it's true. But he only took a small fine from the passengers for ridin' the trains of the Curtain Rail Lines. He was always courteous and polite, and never once so much as inflicted a scratch on no passenger. He even tried to help poor folks around Whistle Stop, 'specially people who lost their ranches to the rail line—like your folks—by seeing to it that some of the loot got to them. Then recently he turned real mean, robbin' and shootin' passengers. Vicious. See what I mean, Jim?"

"People do change, Glen."

Glen slaps his hand on the table. "But a 360 degree turnabout? Only one I knowed that done that so completely was that Dr. Jekyll and Mr. Hyde, and that was only in a book."

Jim is looking at his poker hand. "Hit me for two."

Glen deals two cards to Jim, glances at his hand, and deals three for himself. Jim asks him, "What's your bet?"

"A buck."

Jim closes his hand. "Okay, and I'll raise you another buck."

"You're a real good bluffer, Jim."

"Meet me and see if I am."

"I know you are. I'm out." Glen tosses his cards down on the table. "Let's see what you got."

Jim lays his cards down face up. He has three aces and a pair of queens. "See, it wasn't a bluff at all."

Glen looks closely at Jim. "Y'know something, Jim, the *first* Arizona Adams was something like that hand of yours. As far as

I'm concerned, he was aces." Their eyes meet and his look lets Jim know that Glen knows the truth. "Yes, he was aces with me, and he always will be!"

Chapter 32

Later that week, Jim, still wearing a head bandage, gets off the Curtain Rail Lines train in Jersey City, and enjoys the ferry ride over to New York City. He takes a horse and carriage and watches all of the busy people along the big, broad avenues and streets that take him to the Beagle & Cratchit office building near Central Park. He pays the carriage driver and enters.

The secretary ushers Jim in like a conquering hero. The voice of Mr. Beagle is heard once again greeting him, from behind the huge mahogany desk. "Hello, how are you? How was your trip. How's your head? How's . . ."

Jim holds out his hand. "Howdy, Mr. Beagle. Everything's fine." Mr. Beagle shakes it and then sits down.

"Well, there's no question about it now, Mr. Courtney. You certainly have fulfilled Mr. Curtain's proviso." He pulls a file folder out of a desk drawer and places it on the desk in front of Jim. Handing him a pen, he says, "Just sign and the Curtain Rail Lines company is yours."

Jim signs the paper.

Beagle looks over his signature. "Congratulations, Mr. Courtney! That wraps it up."

"Not quite."

Beagle is surprised. "Not quite?"

"No. I have a proviso of my own."

"What is your proviso?"

"Provided that I have the authority to fire Albert Beamish."

"You have the authority."

"And to cancel all of the pending mortgage foreclosures in and around Whistle Stop. Also, all passengers who were forced to pay fines must be reimbursed. Please advertise that in all the national newspapers. And all westward expansion is to be done only with grants of federal lands."

"Just issue your orders, Mr. Courtney, and your instructions will be followed to the letter."

"Very well, Mr. Beagle, then those *are* my orders."

*

A week later, at the Whistle Stop train station, Ellen is standing on the platform looking eagerly and impatiently up the tracks. As she watches, she hears the sound of the train whistle. Then the train rounds the bend in the distance and grows larger and larger, the whistle sounding over and over as the train slows down and jerks to a stop at the station. Ellen nervously watches two passengers leave the train. Then Jim steps down. Ellen runs down the platform to him and throws herself into his arms. Jim swings her around and they kiss. The train starts to pull out of the station. Henry Parnell and his fellow conductor, who laughed at Jim on his first trip to New York, stick their heads out of the window and wave to Jim and Ellen.

Henry Parnell calls out, smiling widely, "So long, boss! See ya soon."

The second conductor waves and laughs, "And don't worry, we'll take good care of your trains for you!"

They keep waving goodbye while Jim and Ellen continue kissing. The train gathers speed and the whistle sounds again and again as the train recedes in the distance.

That Saturday the banner headline on the front page of *The Whistle Stop Gazette* is:

NEW OWNER OF CURTAIN RAIL LINES MARRIES ELLEN WILLIAMS